# The

# Crew

## By A.W. Mason

Arrow Pig Press, Tampa, FL

First paperback edition October 2022

*Cover Design by Artzy Marz*

ISBN 9798835772056 (Paperback)

Published By Arrow Pig Press

*For Tom, I think he would have liked this one…*

# The World, the Way It Is

The group on the sixth hole didn't see the lumbering bull gator, nor did they see what the old dinosaur had in its mouth. Back on the tee box, a short, squat man lined up his shot and swung his driver at the little white ball. His coral-colored polo clung to his body, thoroughly soaked through by the second hole.

"About shanked that one, didn't you Mitch?" Mr. Coral Polo's cart partner said. The man took a long pull from a can of beer then offered Mitch his own. Mitch accepted the cool can. Condensation dripped from the bottom like the fat drops of sweat cascading from his bulbous red nose.

"I only come out here to drink, Jenkins. You guys are the fools that keep inviting me," Mitch said, getting into the golf cart. "Come on, let's catch up to those other two morons."

Jenkins navigated the cart path and parked under the shade of a massive oak. Spanish moss floated down in the lazy breeze like a faux snowfall. Mitch swatted at the moss and stepped out of the golf cart, the vehicle giving an audible creak of relief.

"Your shot, Mitch," one of the two morons said from the fairway. "I'd go with a four iron here but let's make it interesting. I'll give you a hundred bucks if your ball goes farther than your divot!"

Chuckling, Jenkins finished his beer and worked on relighting his cigar. Mitch grabbed a four-iron from his bag and trudged up to the fairway. He let the club fall between his knees as he set his feet, sweeping the manicured Bermuda grass with each practice stroke. The breeze had all but stopped and the air began to feel like soup.

Mitch reared his club back as a burst of excitement ruffled out of a plot of palm scrub to his left. The foursome turned their heads in unison at the source of the sound. The bull gator swaddled out of the brush, meandering along in front of them. They had caught up to the beast without knowing it was ever there. In its mouth, most of the top half of a man dangled with each step it took forward.

"Shoot, Mitch. I'll throw in another hundred bucks if you can play a carom off the gator too!" Jenkins said.

The gator left a grisly path of sticky blood as the dead man's entrails dragged across the grass like a macabre paintbrush. A golf visor tumbled off the corpse, resting in a pile of gore the gator had created as the creature angled toward a retention pond across the course.

"Should we wait until it's gone or just play through?" Mitch asked, wiping a hand across his sweaty brow.

Jenkins looked back to the tee box. The foursome behind them had caught up. Their golf cart looked like a toy in the distance but they were close enough. "Better play through, buddy."

Mitch nodded and reset his feet, dropping the club between his knees once again. He took one last look at the gator, who had about made it to the cart path, then shifted his gaze to the ball, reared back and swung.

# Chapter 1

I might be the only human in the world who sees someone dying and thinks about what I could do to help save them. I only think about it though. I never help. I want to fit in, I want to be normal.

Just yesterday I saw a woman face down in her phone, take a step off the sidewalk and into the passing 5:15 bus. Her shoes, with her feet still in them, came to a rest half a block from the impact. Did I want to yell out to her? Did I want to warn her about being splattered across the front end of a transit vehicle? Yes, I did. But I didn't. I want to fit in, I want to be normal.

Instead, the 5:15 continued on as bits and pieces of the woman slid off the bus grill, leaving little scraps of flesh like gruesome breadcrumbs. Cleaning her up must not have been too high of a priority. The next day I still saw parts of the woman plastered to the bus bench when I went into the coffee house a block away from the transit stop.

I come here every Wednesday to treat myself to a black iced coffee. I hate it here, this coffee shop. Time speeds up. You lose it. You lose yourself. I really only come here to leave my shithole apartment for a while, especially now that summer is here and it normally feels like an oven in my living room.

I stand in the line, waiting for the barista to translate orders like some sort of court stenographer. There's a man, third in line and I see him start to sway. He falls onto the smooth oak floor—original to the building, constructed in the early 20th century—and starts to convulse. Foamy spittle coalesces at the corners of his mouth as his arms flail into the other customers in line.

The barista calls for the next customer and we all move forward. The lady in front of me steps over the convulsing man, his movements slow and sporadic, then I step forward too. No one looks down at the man. No one acknowledges him. *Yet*. His expensive tie sticks to his cheek, glued there by his own saliva. He'll stay where he is for now until the corpse becomes a nuisance. Then someone will call a Cleanup Crew to remove the body and scrub the area down like nothing ever happened. I know this because I have done this before. I know this because I work for a Cleanup Crew.

You're probably asking yourself how I got so lucky. There are two ways to become employed by the Crew and my path was through the orphanage. My mother died during childbirth and my father died by suicide. Thus, I lived a full life of bouncing around foster homes as nothing more than someone's paycheck. I aged out, never got adopted and at that point, I had two options: join the military and kill people for a living or join the Crew and cleanup dead people instead.

The second way to become a teamster for the Crew is by being deemed a plight on society. Think of your not quite criminally insane or your "high functioning" handicaps; your dishonorably discharged military members; your severely under-educated.

I've been on the same crew for the better part of a decade and lucky enough for me, we are mostly cordial. There's Lefty who is missing his left arm, had been since birth, and no one knows what his actual name is. Then there's Horatio, removed from military service for reasons he keeps secret. We also have Tara, she's the oldest and this is her fourth crew. Then finally, my favorite, Jessie who is a sweet southern girl who likes sweet tea and baking sweet treats to share with us. This suits me just fine since I have a sweet tooth.

Our crew works well together and for the most part, gets along, but none of that getting along like sending each other birthday cards every year kind of way. We all have the same two days off and very rarely see each other outside of work, which also suits me just fine. I feel like that's a normal way of looking at work and your coworkers and you know me, I want to fit in, I want to be normal.

# Chapter 1.5

Another thing real quick. I'm sure you're wondering about a world where death doesn't seem to matter. What of all the hospitals for saving people's lives? What of all the police officers protecting and serving the community in ways that are (supposed) to keep us alive? These services still exist. People still give birth, break bones or contract poison ivy—I'll tell you more about the poison ivy later. There are all sorts of non-life-threatening issues to worry about. Things to improve quality of life.

As for policing? Murder is still illegal although I think it's much easier to get away with now if one knows what they are doing.

And what do we do with the bodies? Your guess is as good as mine. I've heard of mass graves or burning fields. They're all just rumors that Crews tell each other. The government doesn't say one way or another. Anyway, back to the story…

# Chapter 2

My cellphone chirped from the bedroom while I was brushing my teeth. I already knew what it was, an address for today's first cleanup. I don't get any other texts or calls aside from work. You might think that's heartbreaking. I think it's heartwarming.

I looked at the phone screen. Bradford Estates. A high-end neighborhood full of old people with more money than they can spend. These kinds of cleanups weren't uncommon. I typed my confirmation, the first of the Crew to do so, and loaded up my backpack with cleaning supplies. It would be about a fifteen-minute bike ride for me so I'd probably get there first. Tara was the only Crew member that owned a car. She brought most of the supplies we needed and we'd all have to wait on her anyway.

The air outside was muggy, even at ten past eight in the morning. I was thankful for the breeze but when I showed up at our location, the bandana I wore on my head was nothing more than a wet sheet.

Indeed, I was the first crew member there and tried the front door to the palatial property. It opened and a rush of sweet, cool air wrapped around my body like an icy blanket. I pushed past the threshold, glad to be out of the heat, and looked around for our first client of the day. To my immediate right sat an all-granite-everything kitchen. The fridge door had been left ajar. Mostly empty bottles of wine stood like dead soldiers on the countertops.

The party continued down the hall and into a grand library room. A string of lacy garments led to an overstuffed leather sofa chair. There, presumably, the master of the estate sat, eyes closed, mouth open and the lap of his robe erect. On the small end table beside him, various blue and pink pills lay scattered in the remnants of a white residue. Thanks to whatever deity presided over this earth that the first cleanup of the day would be an easy one.

Behind the old bastard was a floor-to-ceiling set of shelves jammed packed with paperbacks and hardcovers. I read. That's what I do. It's my hobby. Some people make birdhouses or collect stamps but I like books. I knew it would be stealing to "borrow" a few of these editions. But the early bird gets the worm when he arrives first on scene and more importantly, doesn't get caught.

I ran a finger over a row of hardcovers. A lot of Carl Hiaasen, a great writer of Florida crime fiction, and an author I have read most works by. Below them was a shelf of books on nature, a rare set of non-fiction. But my eyes landed on an old leather-bound volume on farming and I slid it off the shelf for a closer look. The gold inlay and foil stamping were beautiful. Yet, what really caught my attention was the hidden rows of books behind it.

At first, I thought the old man was doubling up on shelf space but the book behind the now empty slot caught my eye quicker than the woman who walked in front of the 5:15. A blazing white spine with a blood-red cross stamped at the top. Then in black type, *The American Red Cross Book of First Aid*.

I mentioned that non-fiction was a rare bird in today's world and that's because much of it had been rounded up and burned, discontinued from print. Most books about history, books about saving lives and survival, burned up in flame. Anything that gave credence to death or how it may be avoided. Gone.

This American Red Cross book was like the whispered-about Anarchist Cookbook and just as illegal. I pulled out the other front-facing books and discovered a whole row of banned writings. An Army field manual guide from the 1950s. Grief counseling for end of life. Books on major surgeries and traumas. Funeral home procedurals.

The row continued. I unshouldered my backpack and peered at the space inside. I want to fit in. I want to be normal. I couldn't take these books. Even though I do think about saving people for no real reason, owning these books could be a death sentence. I thought all this while my hands worked on stuffing my backpack with as many books as would fit. Then I heard the backpack being zipped up, my hands working again to replace the front-facing row of books.

I stepped back and looked at the shelves. They appeared undistributed. All will be well. The backpack felt like an anchor in my hand. A cement block of paranoia.

Of the books I had shuffled back on the shelf, I spotted a hardcover with a deep orange spine. I pulled it out, amazed to see the almost pristine dust jacket of The Catcher in the Rye. Flipping open to the copyright page, my finger ran down the old paper, stopping at the date. 1951. A first edition. I unzipped my pack again and carefully sandwiched the book between two of the others.

"Strippers called it in," said a voice from the entrance of the library.

I jumped, startled at the sound. The figure walked into the room, revealing himself in the light.

"Horatio, I didn't hear you come in," I said.

"Door was already open," Horatio said, making his way toward the body.

How long had he been standing there? Had he seen me stuff my backpack with books?

"Old dude was having a party apparently. Hired the strippers to help him celebrate his late wife's birthday. Sick fuck," Horatio said. He pressed a finger to the white residue on the end table then lifted it to his mouth and rubbed it on his gums. His tongue flicked across his teeth and he closed his eyes. "At the least, the old man had some good shit."

From outside, the creak of a heavy car door being opened floated in through the front of the house. Tara and the others had arrived. Horatio heard them too and quickly pocketed a group of pills next to the dead man.

"Sounds like the rest of the crew is here. Time to get cleaning!" Horatio said, smirking

# Chapter 3

I lucked out. The cleanup was an easy one. No hazmat. No blood or guts. No multiple clients at the same site. We just bagged him and tagged him, called for the wagon then straightened up the library room. But that wasn't why I lucked out. The cleanup was so quick that I had time to ride back home before our next scheduled job.

The backpack felt like an anchor in the old man's library but as I pedaled back to my apartment, it felt like the Empire State building. The heat had increased. The humidity seemed to double, yet I was in a cold sweat still thinking about what I had taken. At this point I was fairly certain Horatio came in after my transgression. And if not, I doubt he cared about what I was doing after he found the old man's goodies.

My apartment wasn't an ideal place to keep my contraband but it would have to do until I could get it moved to a more secure location. The thought of having to move the books more than once didn't sit well with me. But I had already committed the crime and somewhere under the layers of guilt and fear was a sense of excitement. Being able to read the content between the covers of each volume awoken something within me.

The government didn't pay me well (surprise, surprise) so I didn't have a summer home to stash my loot at. Not even a storage unit. And that was actually fine because those places could have been traced back to me anyway. But I did have a spot. A spot where I wouldn't be bothered and the books wouldn't be disturbed. I just needed time to get them there.

I fished my apartment key from around my neck, jangling it in the lock for purchase when my neighbor's door swung open. Kaitlin. She was on a Crew as well and earned the nickname Killer Kate because word on the street was that she murdered people so that her Crew had a chance for the cleanup. I didn't buy it.

"Hey boy, what are you doing home so early? Not enough work out there for your Crew?" she asked.

"Hi, Kaitlin," I said, still trying to get my key into the deadbolt. "I just came home to change. It's a hot one this morning and we haven't been assigned a new call so far."

She leaned against her doorframe, arms folded, eyeing my backpack as I finally got the key to take.

"They are really starting to stuff y'all's cleanup bags. Don't know how you get around on your bike with that pack," she said.

I turned the lock then worked the handle and pushed the door open. A blast of hot air greeted my already sweaty body. I threw the pack inside.

"Just some extra supplies. Supposed to be a busy week," I said, stepping into my apartment and hoping she'd go back in hers.

"Heard that too, maybe. Heard the Oatley area has been a hotspot."

"Thanks for the heads up. Enjoy your day off, Kaitlin," I said, managing to get inside and the door closed behind me. I heard her door close soon after and I let my breath out.

The pack lay on the living room floor, looking back at me like a mistreated child. I grabbed three cereal boxes from above the fridge, removed the plastic bags and stuffed them in the cabinet. All but two books fit into the empty boxes. Those larger volumes I hid in the bedroom air conditioning vent that hadn't pumped out cool air in years.

While in the bedroom I peeled off my soaked-through shirt and toweled off, standing in front of my fan to cool down. I didn't want to get ahead of myself but it felt like mission accomplished—at least part one—until I had to move the books again to my secure site. I'd do that on my day off, masquerading it as running errands.

My phone chirped again, from my pocket this time. I retrieved the device and looked at the screen. Multiple cleanups in the Oatley district. Killer Kate was right.

# Chapter 4

Two weeks ago, I stuffed my backpack full of banned books. Since then, I'd removed them from my apartment and brought them to my safe place. I'd gone back twice to read the Red Cross first aid book and, as I expected, my contraband was still safe in hiding.

I wondered about the old man, about why he had all these illegal books. About what he did with them or if there was something else going on. I decided I was going to look him up. Against my better judgment, I decided that's what I was going to do. Getting out of my own way has never been a strong point of mine. The only problem? We don't get client information like medical history, let alone names. None of the good stuff. Just an address and the dispatcher's name if we were lucky. We don't even know how the client perished until we get there. Be prepared for anything, Tara always says.

But the old man did my work for me. Inside *The Catcher in the Rye* was a stamp that read "From the Library of Wallace O'Malley" right there on that perfectly unmolested title page. I get it. A bibliophile cherishes their books like their own flesh and blood. But who horses around and puts a goddamn stamp like that inside of an immaculate first edition of such a rare book? Wallace O'Malley does, that's who. Still, I couldn't stand to look at it. He must have really got a bang out of marking such a fine edition, too. That's what absolutely kills me.

A quick internet search told me that old Wallace was a bit of a recluse, much like Salinger himself. He made his fortunes in the tech industry but little else was known about the horny hermit. Yet, there had to be more to the story. My search didn't reveal anything about his clandestine collection, but any man with a library of banned material like that had a story to tell. I just needed to find the storyteller. This would involve going over to see Killer Kate.

I knocked on her door, half hoping she wouldn't answer. But a few seconds later, Kaitlin stood in the open doorway looking me up and down, raising an eyebrow.

"Hello," she said.

I stood in the hallway, backed a few feet away from her trying to figure out how to word my request.

"Well, what is it then, Ethan?"

I swallowed and spoke. "I need your help."

She led me into her apartment and motioned for me to take a seat on the couch. I had only been in here once before when I needed to borrow some supplies after a particularly messy cleanup. Her apartment mirrored mine and was just about as barren.

"You want a drink?" she asked, grabbing a beer out of her fridge.

"No thanks. Actually, I was hoping you could help me research a…a relative of mine. Kind of an outsider. But I found out recently he was related to my birth mother," I told her, hoping she'd buy my story. Not ask too many questions.

Kaitlin opened her beer and drank half the bottle in three giant gulps. She covered her mouth to suppress a burp.

"What's his name?"

"Well, you see, that's sort of private. He was kind of the black sheep of the family," I said.

"A black sheep? In your family? You don't say," she said, finishing the beer. She went back to the fridge and grabbed another. "Just search him on the internet then." She popped the bottle cap off the second beer and danced it across her knuckles. It was sort of hypnotizing.

"Not much about him on there. I heard you knew a way around that though. Some sort of backdoor dark-web business." You see, Kaitlin had what you'd call a reputation for such things.

The bottle cap continued its moves across the back of Kaitlin's hand. She said nothing for a while, making me even more nervous than when I had knocked on her door. Finally, she flipped the bottle cap into the air and caught it in her hand. She slammed it down on the countertop. I jumped.

"I know plenty of things, Ethan. What's in it for me?"

I was afraid she'd ask that.

"What do you want? I don't really have much."

She walked over and sat right in my lap. Her heat-baked thighs stuck to my own like searing leather. She put her arms around my neck, still grasping the beer bottle. The cool glass actually didn't feel too bad on my back.

"Kiss me," she said, leaning into my face.

Kiss her? I didn't have a choice. I was only a little bigger than she was, but she was much stronger. She smacked her lips into mine, parting them with her tongue. Her breath tasted like the cloying malt of lager. It was hot too, like everything else in this forsaken city. I wasn't sure what to do so my tongue sat there in her mouth like a dead fish. She didn't seem to mind or notice.

As soon as it began it was over. *Thank God.* She leaned back and finished her beer, again suppressing a belch after she swallowed. Then she got up as if nothing ever happened and went back into her kitchen, grabbing a scrap of paper.

On the windows, there was this sort of tinted film that kept Kaitlin's apartment a bit cooler than mine. An archaic form of air conditioning I suppose. She scribbled something on the paper and brought it over.

"Here," she said, handing it to me. "Go to this web address and do your search. Make sure to use a VPN or something to cloak your IP address. If you tell anyone where you got this information, I'll kill you."

I believed her.

"Now get the hell out of here before I change my mind," Killer Kate said.

Back in my apartment, I fired up the old laptop again and followed her instructions. I was fairly confident I did everything correctly and that I wasn't being tracked. I didn't have a VPN but who would want to keep tabs on me anyway? The dark-web was something I had always heard about but never experienced. I had no need to. On it, I discovered I could get farm-raised manatee steaks imported from Florida. I found multiple recipes for napalm. I came across listings for dates with an assortment of men and women offering various services.

What I needed though, the information on old Wallace O'Malley, wasn't difficult to find. And man did I ever fall down a rabbit hole. Here's the long and short of it: the man was an eccentric, collecting books at a young age, and he got away with it because his whole family did it. His whole family did it dating back to the Old Years, prior to the way things are now. The years prior to death just being another raindrop in the deluge. His family founded the Alphabet Society, now scarcely referred to and whispered about as the Devil's Alphabet Society. I'd only heard about it in passing. It was something closer to an ancient Greek myth rather than an actual organization.

The Alphabet Society was a group of enlightened people from various communities brought together by their adoration for literature. For years, they amassed libraries full of books regarding every genre. This included all of the banned writings of today. It wasn't until later the Devil's Alphabet Society was formed. They called this time period the Great Shift and it bore such troubling organizations like the Cleanup Crews and the Retribution Squad. After that shift, the Society continued to build its rank of like-minded individuals under the cover of secrecy. Decades later it became a haven for anyone questioning things the way I was. But they also became the number one enemy of the state.

That wasn't even the interesting part though. The interesting part was that this group indeed existed and still exists presently. Reading on, I learned that O'Malley and his brother Willard had continued the secret society until Wallace had a falling out with the group. He chose to live in seclusion with his books and his money, shut off from most of mainline society.

I had to take a break and tuck my head into my freezer to cool down. I swear to God that old laptop put off more heat than the damned sun. My eyes ached from reading and my fingers throbbed from stroking the keys. But before I called it a night, I stumbled upon a chat room, buried deep in the annals of a Devil's Alphabet search. I flip-flopped back and forth at least a half-dozen times about using it. Should I tell them about the books I found at Wallace's place?

For all I knew the Retribution Squad—the death division of the police force—had either infiltrated or created this chat. Maybe posing as the secret society to catch sympathizers and active members. However, I felt like I was already in too deep. I had questions and I wanted answers. I wanted to know if there really were others out there like me. I wanted to know if I really did fit in somewhere. If I really might be normal or that life could blossom into something deeper and more meaningful. Hell, I wanted to know if *death* really was more meaningful.

So, I did it. I reached out. I typed in what I knew, what I had done. I asked if this was all a game or if these books I had really meant something, stood for an alternative way of life. I typed it in the chat box and hit send. Then I closed the laptop and zombie-walked into my stuffy bedroom, laid on the bed and shut my eyes where sleep captured me not long later.

# Chapter 5

I've always been a heavy sleeper. Since I can remember really. I think it's because of the foster system. I never had my own room, usually sharing with two or even three other foster siblings. If I hadn't developed those deep sleeping skills, I bet the chainsaw-like snoring or hours of children bawling for their real parents would have turned me into a somnambulist.

One time, when I was much younger and living close to a fault line, me and two other foster brothers slept through an earthquake. It wasn't one of those really big ones that bring down bridges or anything. But I remember being woke up by my foster mother and seeing a long thin crack that had run up the wall and into the ceiling where the house's foundation had shifted.

I was no heavy sleeper this day though. At around four a.m. almost on the damn dot, a single chime from my computer notified me I had a new message. That got me bolt upright out of bed as if a gong had been dropped on my head. Whatever dream I was having started to fade away like a lifting fog and I reached for my laptop. A message from the Devil's Alphabet Society blinked on the darkened screen. As far as messages go, it was nothing more than a post-it note. There was a general location, a time (5:00 a.m.) and a line under that telling Mr. Ethan Pointe to bring *The Catcher in the Rye*.

I sat in my bed for probably five minutes, reading the message a fourth and fifth time. This is what I wanted, right? I wanted to know about the books, about the man, about this secret society. And I got my answer, sort of. But then again, it also crossed my mind that the whole thing was a hoax, or even worse, a setup. I had no reason to believe it wasn't a Retribution Squad looking for potential offenders, people questioning the way things were these days. Questioning normalcy.

So, I got up, got dressed and headed for the door, pausing one last time to consider how stupid this might all turn out. I might never set foot in this shitty rat-hole apartment again. But I took a deep breath, pushed open my door then locked it behind me.

Outside it was still dark, and even though it was summertime, the sun still wouldn't begin to rise for a few more hours. I decided to walk since it was still relatively cool out and the meeting coordinates were not far from my apartment building. As I trudged along, getting closer and closer, my mind went back to old Wallace and what he might have been up to all those years ago, what his *real* story was.

And if I was paying more attention to my surroundings and not thinking of that old bastard, I probably would have noticed the van creeping up behind me, lights off. I probably would have noticed the man hanging out of the sliding side door with the hood in his hands. What I did notice was the purplish darkness around me going entirely black again, my sight obstructed by a starchy burlap material. And then I was pulled into something, swept from the street like I was another man that just dropped dead and ceased to exist. Here one minute, gone the next.

# Chapter 6

The sack over my head smelled faintly of cat shit. I wondered if it had ever been washed. I had to move both of my hands up to my face to maneuver the cloth away from my nose as my captors had decided to zip tie my wrists together. As the van started to roll to a stop a few minutes later, its occupants began to talk.

"Holy shit. He actually has it," a man said.

"How do we not it's not a fake? Or forged?" a woman responded.

A different man answered. "It's real. I'd know my brother's handwriting anywhere."

Ah, must be good old Willard. The man himself.

My vision came back to me in a sudden rush of dull light as the woman removed my veil. She was sitting across from me on the floor of the van which had no seats. Next to her was the other man and across from him, Willard I assumed, who was examining *The Catcher in the Rye*.

"Tell us again how you got it," the woman said. And so, I did.

Willard closed the book and looked up at me. He was smiling, the kind smile that used to cross my face while daydreaming about being adopted. Willard was quite a bit younger than his deceased brother but there was no denying the relation.

"I haven't seen this book in ages. We both got a copy, from our parents. Only I lost mine some years back. Wallace was always so much better with his books back then," Willard said.

"How do we know he's not Retribution?" the other man asked.

My ass was starting to go numb from sitting on the van's bare steel. It was about as comfortable as perching on a wrought iron fence.

"Me? I thought you guys would probably be Retribution posing as sympathizers to get me off the grid. I guess at this point it doesn't really matter," I said.

"Listen," Willard said. We all paused.

"I don't hear anything," the woman said.

"You're right. And if our friend here was on the Squad we would have been surrounded by now. At the very least we would have been chased," Willard said. He drew a knife and brought it toward me. "Sorry. Never can be too cautious."

I closed my eyes expecting to feel a sharp, hot bloom in my midsection. Or maybe the steel of the blade plunging between my ribs. Instead, Willard cut the zip ties binding my wrists and threw them next to the odorous head sack. The ties weren't too tight, thankfully, but enough to where I had to rub my wrists until they felt normal again.

"You'll have to forgive my associates. They really do mean the best. We've been on the hook before, almost exposed. It's not a great feeling," Willard said. He was still wearing that nostalgic smile.

"I understand," I said. Trying to swallow was like trying to force a softball into a teacup. The atmosphere, though, seemed to be getting less tense. "How'd you know it was me? I mean, how'd you know I was Ethan?"

"The book in your hand was a pretty good indicator," the woman said.

"We owe you some introductions. This man over here is Dave Floyd. Across from you is Isabell Cabrera. As you have probably figured out, I'm Willard O'Malley."

Willard stuck his hand out and shook mine with gentle force.

"What about him?" I asked, motioning to the driver.

The van members looked toward the front and a large, stubble-headed man turned toward us. He had a shy smile and dark eyes.

"Oh, that's Lenny," Willard said. Lenny waved.

Dave leaned over and took the book from Willard and stuffed it into a backpack. He had a glistening layer of sweat printed on his brow. Even at this hour, the heat started to turn up.

"So, it's all real then. You guys. The Devil's Alphabet Society," I said.

"So, they call us," Isabell chimed in. From the front of the van came a tapping sound as Lenny drummed on the steering wheel. He looked out the van's windshield, scanning the darkness, probably for some lookey-loos wondering what kind of party was going on inside the vehicle.

"I never did like that name, but yes. We're real. And as you can attest to, maybe not the easiest thing to find. We're okay with just being a whisper in the wind to most people.

It wasn't always like that. My family has been at this for years but the Age of Enlightenment is, unfortunately, becoming a thing of the past," Willard said.

"Age of Enlightenment?" I asked.

"The time before, when death mattered and people mourned," Willard replied.

Everything, so far, that I had read on the dark web was true. That excited me but in a way that churned my stomach a bit. I started to wonder if I was getting myself into something that I shouldn't be. This was no way to contribute to the façade of being normal. But, like my hands reaching for Wallace's banned books, my mind reached out to the Society for more information.

"Then there's a place, a place that people can go and be free thinkers like us," I said.

"Freethinkers like *us*," Dave said, waving an arm to his companions, cutting me out.

Willard smiled at the notion. I felt like he hadn't stopped smiling since he had seen that book.

"We have a place," he said, "where all like us are welcomed. But we have to be careful. You've done your research. However, so have many other people interested in the idea of life and death but have no intention of expanding upon it. Changing it."

Lenny's drumming went into something that might have been from Rush.

"But we also don't get many people willing to risk meeting up with us. After all, we're known felons now. America's most wanted, perhaps," Willard continued.

"I see death every day. I make it disappear as easily as the people who just ignore that it happens. I do it because it's my job. I do it because I have to, it's my assignment. But I never understood why," I said.

Yes, it was definitely Rush.

"So then, that leads us to our next question. What do you want to do about it?"

I pondered Willard's inquiry. I had never really thought about that part of it. Was I curious? Sure. Did any of it sit well with me? Not one bit. Did I want to help people and guide others' ways of thinking, change the deadly dynamic that had been in place for years and years and years? I wasn't entirely sure.

"I want to help." My mouth apparently made my decision for me. "But I don't know how."

"Are you willing to leave your life behind? Possibly your family and friends? Can you survive in the knowledge that you're not another pawn in a scheme to perpetuate the groupthink that plagues the human race?" Isabell asked.

Rush turned into The Who. Baba O'Riley.

"I don't know. I have a pretty awesome apartment," I said.

The group stared at me. Even Lenny.

"It was a joke. Sorry, I'm not great at jokes," I said.

"This is no joke, Ethan," Dave said.

"I don't have a family. I don't have anyone I'd consider a friend. I'm on a Crew for a reason. My parents died and I was orphaned. I do the same thing day in and day out. I contribute, in a way I suppose, to the problem. It doesn't feel right to me."

Keith Moon started up again.

"Whatever you're asking of me. I think I can do it. I think I'm in," I said.

"It's not that easy," Isabell said.

Willard found his smile again, that sweet, sweet smile. He should have been a grief counselor or something. As if we really had a need for those anymore.

"I suppose there is sort of an…" Willard started, waving his hand around as he thought, "…an initiation so to say. Dave, show him."

Dave rolled up a sleeve on his right arm. Even in the scant light, I could see the gruesome scar tissue of a major burn. It traveled up from his wrist and disappeared into his shirt.

"I ran into a house fire. I pulled out two children. By the time I could reach their parents, they were both dead from smoke inhalation," Dave said.

"Isabel?" Willard asked.

"My best friend was overdosing. Fentanyl. I injected her with Narcan."

"Narcan? How the hell did you come across some Narcan?" I asked her.

"When you're a junkie, you can get pretty much anything when you put your mind to it," she replied. Her eyes dropped to her hands in her lap.

"And you?" I asked Willard.

"I've been saving people for years, I guess you might say. It's been a family business since before I was born. I save anyone who needs saving. I think you need that saving, Ethan."

Outside a car roared past on its way to who knows where. We all looked in the direction of the sound, holding our collective breaths until it passed.

"What about him?" I asked, nodding my head to Lenny. He transitioned into another old song, My Hero.

"We recruited Lenny before he could be equalized by a Retribution Squad. Some people accept their deaths even after being saved. And then some, like our friend here, know that it doesn't have to be like that. Shouldn't be like that," Willard said.

My head swam with their stories, with the information about Wallace and the books I had stashed away.

"How will you know I've done it? Saved someone. How will I know where to go?" I asked.

"We will know. And here," Willard said handing me a piece of scrap paper. On it was a phone number, nothing else. "You'll call us when you need to find us."

"And you'll know it's me," I said looking at the scrap paper, not really asking the question but wondering about it instead.

"You'll need to know the code words. We won't write those down for you in case that paper falls into the wrong hands. And your code words will only work for you," Willard said.

I looked up from the paper and into Willard's eyes. His smile had disappeared. He leaned over, close to my face.

"Remember these words. He thrusts his fists against the posts and still insists he sees the ghosts."

I nodded my head and repeated the phrase over and over again to myself.

"Now I'll have to apologize, we need to get on and we are going to have to part ways. I'm confident you will find your way back from here, yes?" Willard said.

I nodded again and with that exited the van, watching the Devil's Alphabet Society speed away.

# Chapter 7

It's a Tuesday. It's my day off. The whole clandestine meet-up slash abduction—whatever you want to call it—seemed more and more like a dream as time passed. I thought about it, the invitation into the Devil's Alphabet Society. I really did. I just didn't know if I could pull the trigger. Okay, that's probably not the right wording. Pulling triggers doesn't typically equate to saving lives.

Since it was my day off and nearing triple digits on the Fahrenheit scale, I decided to leave my hotbox apartment and ride down to the city pool. Technically named Dowding pool, after some county diplomat, people referred to it as Drowning pool. Cute, I know. I'm not the biggest fan of the place. Too many people. Too many kids running around screaming at each other while their parents sip iced wine from concealed water bottles. Too many testosterone-filled teenage boys doing tricks from the diving board, trying to impress the teenage girls laying out in the sun. It all seemed like some sort of archaic mating ritual.

But the water was cool enough to make me forget about the sun filling up my apartment with the heat of a thousand volcanoes so I deal with the people. And it's closer than the beach by about twenty minutes. I don't really like the beach either. The sand gets everywhere and it's almost impossible to get rid of. Plus, I was there a month or so ago when my Crew got called out to remove the body of a young woman who had overdosed. Whoever she was with had the courtesy to cover her up with a beach towel. Touching.

So anyway, I don't come to the pool very often. Drowning was a leading cause of death in many infants and children and not having lifeguards on duty, it's just something I have to push to the back of my mind. Otherwise, I might end up getting heat stroke while sitting on my couch.

I parked my bike, paid the entrance fee and walked into the shallow end of the pool. It was like stepping into a people-infested haven. Although, luckily, on Tuesdays the pool didn't hit max capacity. There were still more people than I cared for but I was able to carve out my own space in the deep end and relax for a while.

I stayed in long after my fingers turned pruney. People say that's an indication that you're in the water too long. It's not. It's just the body's natural reaction to being submerged in liquid. The ridges on your fingertips help to grip things better under wetter circumstances. That's all. I learned that from reading a portion of the wilderness survival guide I had stowed away at my safe place.

The sun reached its apex in the cloudless sky and I scanned the pool to see if any of my Crew was there. Not that I'd go over and hold a conversation with them or anything. I was just curious to see if they might be struggling with the heat like I was. But, alas, I did not recognize any of the faces applying sunscreen, doing cannonballs or ordering chicken fingers from the concession stand. Fine with me.

The time was right to start thinking about getting back home. I probably had time to visit the safe place as well which put me in a better mood. There's only so much screaming and laughing and splashing and yelling for help that I can take.

Wait. Yelling for help?

I scanned the pool again. There in the far part of the deep end, among a throng of fully capable adults, a woman bobbed up and down on the chlorinated surface. Her hands thrashed violently for something solid to pull herself up with. She screamed again only to have it muffled as her head sunk below the waterline.

The people around her continued to slap an inflatable beach ball at each other, hee-hawing it up. On one particular volley, the ball hit the drowning woman in the face before careening toward a man with swim goggles wrapped around his fat head. The diving board continued to provide its ephemeral entertainment to those lined up to use it and all around the woman, life went on.

Well, except for the woman's life as her struggles became weaker, her head appearing above the water less and less. She was going to die. And no one would help her. I want to fit in. I want to be normal.

It was like when my hands just started grabbing the books off the old dead man's shelves. My mind contemplated the action, even dismissing it as something wrong, but there those hands were. You know, grabbing hardcovers and paperbacks and stuffing them into my bag. It was like that because, by the time I recited my personal mantra (I want to fit in. I want to be normal), I had already swum over to her spot in the deep end. I smacked the beach ball out of the way as I made it to the drowning woman, the Devil's Alphabet Society the furthest thing from my mind.

I grabbed her under her arms, the buoyancy of the water helping me guide her to the edge of the pool like we were on a conveyor belt. The woman weighed no more than 115 pounds soaking wet—which I suppose she was—making it easy work to get her up on the concrete next to the diving board. I, myself, wasn't too much bigger so the water may have been more of a life preserver than I was.

The woman, who seemed to be around my age, maybe early thirties at the oldest, lay unresponsive with her legs still dangling in the water of the pool. I pushed myself out of the deep end and kneeled next to her lifeless body. Maybe I was too late. I laced the fingers of my hands into a solid mass and found the center of the woman's chest, sliding down to the end of the sternum. That's what it said to do in the Red Cross book.

Then I'm supposed to push down and let my arms work back up and repeat that motion for at least 100 beats per minute. I can then pinch the nose, slightly tilt the head back, create an airtight seal around her mouth with mine and blow two short bursts of oxygen into her lungs. Then back to the compressions.

This all went through my head as I set my hands on her chest but what I didn't see, what I didn't realize at first was the stillness. The stillness of the people in the pool, their eyes on me like lasers, their eyes wide like inflatable beach balls. The stillness of the water as all the diving and cannonballs ceased. The stillness of the air when the children quit screaming, now preoccupied with the man and the woman at the deep end of the pool. Even the breeze seemed to stop.

I looked up, hands still on the woman's sternum, waiting to start the CPR.

"Shit," I said.

"Shit is right," the woman said, leaning up on her elbows as she surveyed the stunned crowd. "And get your hands off me."

She was alive. Did I save her? I mean, I pulled her out of the water and stopped her from drowning. I didn't get a chance to perform CPR but I saved her. Right? So much for being normal. So much for fitting in. Goodbye personal mantra.

"We need to get out of here. Now," the woman said as she eyed the pool people, frozen like statues. She was right. You don't hear about it very often. People trying to save people. It's just not the societal norm. And after years and years and decades and decades of living this way, evolution kind of took over. If you believe in that sort of thing. I did.

We got up and trotted toward the shallow end of the pool and to the exit. I grabbed my backpack from the lounge chair near the concession stand. The pool people statues all turned their heads to watch us as we made an advance toward the parking lot. How long would it take them to snap out of this trance? How long would it take someone to call in a rescue attempt, a thwarted death?

"Do you have a car?" the woman asked.

"No," I replied. "Do you?"

"Nope, took the bus," she said, squeezing her eyes shut as if she were experiencing a migraine. "I assume you did the same?"

"No, I have a bicycle. I rode my bicycle."

"Great," she said, reaching behind her to grab my hand so I could keep up with her pace. "Can you balance the two of us until we get clear of this place?"

"Yes, I think so," I said as I unlocked my bike from the rack. I pulled the shoes from my pack and slipped them on. "My apartment is close. We can go there and figure out what to do. I'm Ethan, by the way."

"I don't care who the fuck you are," she said. "Let's just get on your bike and ride."

# Chapter 8

I hate being a burden to people. I remember once in second grade, my class was outside for recess. I was sitting on a railroad tie that created a border for the playground while my classmates traversed the monkey bars and rocketed down the slide. My teacher was standing over by me and a few other loner kids, talking to some new faculty. My arms were stretched out to my sides, resting on the railroad tie, when my teacher stepped back and her foot landed on top of my hand.

I didn't yell out or scream in pain. I was hoping she'd just step off and stop crushing all my little phalanges so we could just forget this little incident ever occurred. Instead, she finally looked down during a break in the conversation and saw where her foot was. She stepped off immediately and in a scolding tone asked why I didn't tell her I was under her foot.  It was okay, I told her. I didn't want to be a burden.

Sitting on the couch in my living, the drowning woman was giving me the same scolding look as my teacher. I let her borrow some of my clothes which were a tad baggy on her but were at least dry. We pedaled back to my apartment without incident. I'm pretty sure we got inside my building undetected. The only thing I could think of to do now was to lay low and see what happened next.

"Why didn't you just let me drown? I was supposed to drown," she said as she paced the small living room.

"I'm sorry. But you were screaming for help," I said.

She continued to storm through the apartment, eyes on the floor, maybe trying to come up with a plan that would get her out of the trouble I put her in.

"You know how the world works, Ethan. People die and we just let them. That's the way it is. The way it always will be. But now I'm standing here *alive* in your crappy little apartment. We're both screwed. You know that, right?"

I did, of course. Plenty of people saw me this time. And if there were cameras at the pool then we would most likely make the afternoon news. Fugitives on the run. A real Bonnie and Clyde in reverse.

"Look, I know you are mad at me but it was just a reflex. I didn't even know I was doing it until I had pulled you out of the pool. Again, I'm sorry. I know that doesn't mean anything but maybe this will all blow over," I said.

Her eyes shot up from the floor and bore into me like an oil rig. Outside the sun still blazed, creating a pale-yellow beam from my kitchen window.

"You're mad if you think this thing is just going to go away. Trying to save someone is the equivalent of manslaughter. Even worse if you would've tried a lifesaving technique. I can tell by looking at you though; you're no surgeon. You wouldn't even pass for a lifeguard."

She was right about the surgeon part. She was right about all of it. Prison had air conditioning, or so I've been told, so maybe it wouldn't be so bad to be caught after all. But, had

I been caught in the process of administering CPR, that would have been like a murder charge at that point.

The woman stepped into the kitchen and opened the fridge. At first, I thought she was trying to find some relief from the heat as I've often done, but instead, she pulled out a bottle of beer, popped the top and began to chug. Small streams of golden lager ran down from her mouth and trailed along her slick pale neck. When she finished the beer, she let out a sizeable belch and smashed the bottom of the bottle on the countertop, creating some sort of shank. She held the jagged glass to her neck.

"Hey, hey! Wait. What are you doing?" I knew what she was doing.

"I was supposed to die in that pool. I'm just remedying the situation now. I'll puncture my jugular and drown in my own blood instead. It's the only way to fix this," she said.

I tried not to make any sudden movements. My hands stretched out toward her in case she actually plunged the bottle into her neck.

"You're here now. You're alive. It must be for some reason. Death isn't supposed to be like this. Please, just tell me your name," I said.

"Yeah, I'm here now because you saved me. Why do you want to know my name so bad if I'm just going to be dead on your apartment floor in a few seconds?"

The woman pressed the glass harder into her flesh. A small trickle of blood oozed from a cut and flowed like runny syrup down the broken bottle.

"Please," I begged, sitting up from the couch.

"It's Luci," she said with a loud sigh. "Do you mind if I drive this broken bottle into my neck now?"

"I would prefer that you didn't. I think I know how to stop the bleeding and sew you back up but I don't have the supplies for it."

Luci cocked her head to one side, shooting me a curious glance. The tension from the bottle on her neck lessened.

"What did you say? You would know how to stitch me back up, huh?"

Well shit. I said too much again. Why did I ever take those stupid books? I couldn't just leave well enough alone. All my life I have tried to blend in with society and limit the exposure to my true feelings. It only takes one simple act to screw it all up. What did it leave me with? A strange woman in my kitchen trying to slash her own throat.

"You know what? Never mind. Please just put the bottle down, Luci. We can figure something out. Together."

"No, really," she said, "tell me what you know about—"

Loud bangs from the door. Muffled voices. We both looked toward the front hallway then back at each other. Sweat dripped from my forehead but my body went cold. My breathing stopped.

"Open up! We know you're in there!" a voice yelled from the hallway. They found us. So much for laying low and seeing how this might all blow over.

Luci set the bottle down and mouthed at me 'What do we do?' I remained frozen. There was flight or fight, but also there was freeze. That was me. A snowman in a hundred-degree apartment. Not only was I responsible for myself, but now I had Luci to deal with. I'd get my punishment, probably life in prison and more likely death. But they'd also take Luci knowing she was due to expire and complete the job for her. All would be balanced. All would be normal. But hey, she wanted that anyway.

Luci crept over to me and whispered in my ear, "I don't want to die."

Seems I was wrong.

The pounding on the door continued. Next, they would start to kick it in. Then they would drag us out and throw us in the wagon. I could already see my door frame splintering.

"What do we do?" Luci whispered to me, tugging on my shirt. "Where do we go?"

What do we do? Where do we go? What do we do? Where do we go? Oh, I knew a place. A safe place. A place I have never shown anyone. But Luci was my responsibility now, my charge.

"Quick," I said. "Put that kitchen chair under the front doorknob. It should buy us a little time. We're going down the fire escape."

Luci obliged. I ran to the window, which was already halfway propped open, and slid it up to access the fire escape. The sunbaked steel railing seared my skin as I grabbed it to pull myself through the window. Luci followed behind me.

"What if they are waiting down there for us too?" she asked, looking at the street below.

"Then we're both going to get a free ride to a bad place."

# Chapter 9

The coast was clear. If anyone was waiting for us down in the street, they didn't get the memo about our descriptions. I liked to think I blended in anyway. There's nothing special about me. I'm average height, average weight or maybe less, unremarkable face. I didn't dress in loud colors or designer jeans; I just couldn't afford to. Simple as that.

Luci though, she had the look of a domineering executive type. All business. She even had that air about her in my cheap plain clothing. She scared me a little, but not in a menacing way. I don't know. I guess it's hard to explain. I just know I'd probably listen to most things she told me to do. Especially now that I knew she didn't want to kill herself.

I pedaled us away from my apartment, past the business district and toward Olde Town. Olde Town was just as it sounded. Hundreds of years ago it was the epicenter of the city. A thriving economic hot spot that, through the years, didn't so much fade away but burnt out. It was still a few steps away from ghetto status but most of the businesses had long since boarded up and moved or dissolved altogether. I liked it here. Not very many people, and the ones you might encounter generally left you alone.

We rode through the streets, past the Dixie Pig BBQ Cafe and past the old Gas N' Go until we reached Purdue Place. A makeshift chain link fence flanked the entire block of Purdue but I knew where a section had been cut away some years back.

"Well, if you didn't want anyone to find us, mission accomplished," Luci said as she hopped off the bike. I watched her as I peeled back the slit in the fence. Her eyes flicked over the decrepit buildings and debris-strewn parking lots, overrun by weeds and trash. I think I saw her shiver.

"After you," I said, holding the chain link back from the opening.

After I got the bike through, concealing it with some rotting wooden pallets, we walked another two buildings over until we reached my safe place. The business sign, which sat atop the front of the building, had been partially covered by an invasive ivy.

Luci looked up and read it aloud. "'Lefton's Fun Home?' What, was this some sort of arcade?"

I smirked and motioned for her to follow me over to the side of the building. The front door had a massive chain wrapped around the handles and a lock bigger than a brick securing it all.

"C'mon. We have to go through this window over here," I said, making a quick look around to make sure we weren't followed. The window slid up with ease, the lock broken years ago, and I pushed myself up and through it. Luci followed suit, nearly slipping on the old linoleum floor inside when she landed.

"It doesn't smell the greatest in here," Luci said, holding her nose.

"Smells like freedom," I responded, making my way to the foyer.

The stale air trapped throughout the building did nothing to alleviate the heat. A thin layer of perspiration blanketed my skin after no longer than a minute. Luci seemed to be in the same sweaty camp but at least she wasn't holding her nose any longer. On the front desk, across from the chained-up entrance, a musty, moth-eaten book sat open. I spun it around toward Luci.

"Would you like to sign in, ma'am?" I asked, presenting her the blotter.

Luci's eyes scanned the header on the open page. "Lefton's Funeral home. So, I guess there aren't any pinball machines in here then?" She walked around the front counter, glancing down the empty hallway to the left. The light came in sparing rays through the grimy, newspaper-ed windows. "I was really looking forward to playing some Centipede or Asteroids."

"This place is better than an arcade. We won't run into anyone here. When was the last time anyone even thought about a funeral parlor?" I asked.

Luci nodded, still exploring the front room. She ran her fingers over the antique couch near the front doors. Motes of dust fluttered into the air as she wiped her hands on her shirt. Well, my shirt but who is really counting at this point? "So this is the place you go when you want to get away," she said, not quite asking. "When you want to hide."

"This isn't even the best part. Follow me," I said, heading around the front desk and through the doors behind it.

We wove around an office, through a break room, and to a door that led to a staircase plunging into the darkness below us. I picked up the kerosene lantern I stored next to the door. This place hadn't had electricity in ages and downstairs there were no windows.

I motioned for Luci to follow, which she did willingly enough. At the base of the stairs, I pushed through a batwing style set of doors. I went around to each of the candles I had set up around the sprawling room, lighting them. Luci stayed at the foot of the stairs watching me, as the warm dancing lights brought the funeral home's morgue to life.

"Welcome to the dead room," I said, spreading my arms out over my kingdom.

Down here, the building was probably thirty degrees cooler, another reason this was my safe place. In the far room, I pulled one of the nine slots in the wall designed to hold and preserve the dearly departed. It made a rather perfect-sized resting bench for someone of my size.

"I have to admit," Luci said, taking it all in, "this is much cooler than an arcade. I've always had a morbid curiosity for things like this. Things like death."

"I could tell," I said, nodding at her neck. A small crimson splotch of blood still stood out on her throat, the sweat not quite washing away that memory. She touched the wound.

"Isn't that how the world is?" she asked.

"The world isn't curious about death. They don't care about it. It doesn't matter to them."

"But it matters to you?"

I stared into the dark ceiling of the morgue. "Well, I'm curious about it, sure," I said.

Luci sidled up to me, propping her elbows up on the cool steel where I lay. Her breath felt inches away.

"But you saved me. Doesn't that mean death matters to you?"

"I told you. It was a reflex, not an instinct."

"And the CPR was a reflex too?"

She had me there. *Again*. What was the point in misleading her? She was in this just as much as I was.

"Do you really feel like being my therapist right now?" I asked.

She moved her face closer to mine. Her hand reached out and covered my chest.

"Show me how to do it. Show me how to save people."

My body shivered, broke out in gooseflesh as her other hand shot out and alit on my sternum.

"Don't be a hypocrite. I believe it was you with the broken bottle to your neck a few short hours ago," I said, eyes still fixed on the ceiling.

"But I changed my mind. Isn't that what humans do when presented with new facts? They make *different*, informed decisions. I don't want to die. I made that pretty clear. I followed you here, didn't I?"

"I don't think you had much of a choice once they found us," I said.

But she was right. Even if the reasoning behind her recent change of heart was founded on fear of apprehension, here was my chance to help somebody that could be like me. Eventually no longer fitting in. Eventually no longer normal.

I opened my mouth to speak this into existence but Luci hopped up and straddled me, her legs hanging off each side of the steel slab. She took her shirt off, the shirt I lent her, exposing her pale bare chest. She wrestled my right hand from behind my head and placed it on her left breast, cupping it, and my hand, with both of hers.

"Show me how to save lives," she whispered into the dim room.

"Actually," I swallowed, "my hand wouldn't go there. Your heart is closer to the sternum." I tried to slide my hand down to the proper CPR location but Luci's strength surprised me. She wouldn't let me move.

My own heart started to beat faster; I could feel the pulse in the side of my neck. Luci leaned over, still forcing my hand to her breast, and spoke into my ear, "Your hand is exactly where it needs to go."

Oh boy, here we go. I knew she was probably just trying to be nice. But all she had to do was say 'Thank You'. She really didn't owe me anything.

"You don't have to do this," I said as I tried to get my left arm out from resting behind my head. "You don't owe me anything."

"Do you think that this is what this is? Payment?"

She leaned up again, letting go of my hand, and threw her head back, laughing like a hyena. The laughter echoed in the cavernous room like some raucous late-night show audience.

"You're right; I don't owe you anything. As I said, I have a morbid curiosity and all of this is, well, it's turning me on," Luci said.

"But there's nothing morbid about saving people's lives. It's really the opposite, isn't it?" I pleaded. It didn't matter though. All this touching, invasion of my personal space. Well, my body reacted the way any teenaged hormone-filled boy would react. Even now as an adult.

"And it's also illegal which gets me going even more," she said while fumbling with my belt clasp. "You trust me, don't you? You know we are in this together."

There was that phrase again. We were already bonded for better or worse based on my actions at the pool. It felt like this was her way of taking action to make the bond just as much hers.

"What's the matter?" she asked, getting my belt free. Her hand undid my zipper. "You've had sex before, haven't you?"

"Of course," I said. It was true too. I was younger, living in one of many group homes. I was thirteen. She was seventeen. I was under the impression the locked door was just so she could talk to me in private, about some mundane school issue maybe. But soon I found myself with my pants around my ankles, and thirty-three seconds later my foster sister dismounted me and told me if I ever said anything about it to anyone, she'd cut my penis off.

"Then relax," Luci said, reaching into my shorts, grabbing my erection. Somehow, with her free hand, she stripped off everything below her waist then navigated herself back on top of what she held in her hand. She swayed her hips back and forth while my eyes remained affixed to the ceiling.

It was comical to think of the stillness and stiffness of my body on the steel slab, where I'm sure hundreds of bodies had been before in such a state. But, if my thirteen-year-old self's average kept up, in twenty-five more seconds this would all be over.

Luci thrust herself forward on me, leaning her head close to my ear again.

"Tell me, Ethan, tell me how to stop death," she breathed into me. "I want to know how to save you."

Maybe if I told her, she'd just stop.

"I want to know how you do it."

Twenty more seconds.

"I want to know how you know."

She started to grind harder. Faster.

"Where did you learn?"

Ten seconds.

"Teach me, Ethan."

I wasn't going to tell. Not ever.

"Oh god, I want you to teach me, Ethan."

Five seconds…

"I have books!" I screamed into the room as I climaxed. My average had apparently dropped. "I have books," I said more hushed as she leaned back up and slowly continued to sway her hips on me.

"What kind of books, Ethan?"

My body started to shiver all over again. I was numb but it was ecstasy.

"First aid. Survival manuals. Medicinal Plants," I sighed.

"Show me."

I showed her

# Chapter 10

The plan was to get something to eat *because* we were both exhausted and famished from the running and fucking. The plan was to sit down and map out our next moves *because* we had no idea what we were doing. The plan was there was no plan *because* we had no idea what we were doing.

After I showed Luci my contraband, which I kept in an old Cleanup Crew backpack from years past, I shoved it back into one of the sliding steel slabs and closed the small square door behind it. It was the best I could do at hiding it in "plain sight".

"How much money do you have?" Luci asked. She was finally putting her clothes back on. My clothes.

I turned out my pockets then removed my wallet. It seemed much warmer down here in the dead room.

"Twenty-two dollars. Fifty-five cents. That's it," I said. I knew she couldn't contribute. All of her things were still back at the pool.

"I'm hungry. We will have to go someplace cheap. Is there anything open close to here?" she asked.

I thought about it. Olde Towne had a few food options but they were the kind of places you went to when you had no money at all. To call them soup kitchens would be like calling a soup kitchen a Michelin-rated restaurant.

"There are some places in the Arrow District, maybe a five-minute bike ride from here," I said.

"Fine," Luci Responded. "Let's go then. My stomach is starting to eat my backbone."

We ended up at a greasy spoon called Mel's Burgerlust. Mel had been dead in his grave (or wherever the Crew that cleaned him up decided to put him) for some years. According to the chatter in the booths around us, Mel took his recipes with him.

A middle-aged man in a stained white apron and oily paper hat came up to take our orders. He licked his thumb and turned to a new sheet on his little paper pad.

"What'll it be?" he asked, eyes fixed on the pad.

"We'll both have waters. And I'll take a side salad with balsamic. You can send it out when his meal comes," Luci said.

I looked over the menu and decided on the corned beef hash since they served breakfast all day. The man with the greasy hat closed his pad and shuffled off toward the kitchen. On his way, he almost knocked down one of the ancient framed posters cluttering each wall in the joint. The server straightened out Humphrey Bogart and slouched into the back of house.

Outside it began to rain, covering up the noise of the clinking spatulas and slamming plates from the kitchen.

"So, where'd you get them?" Luci asked me, playing with the straw in her water. "The books."

"It doesn't matter," I said. "We should be coming up with a plan on what to do next. Where should we go? What should we do? Right?"

Above us, the ceiling fan rattled and gyrated as if trying to detach from the ball and socket that kept it in place.

"It does matter. Perhaps wherever you stole them from can be a place to go to. I imagine that might be some sort of a safe place."

"Doubtful we could go back there. It was just an old man's mansion. He was hiding the books like I am now," I said. "What we need to do is find some more people like him. Like us." I was still a bit hesitant to tell her what I knew about the Devil's Alphabet Society.

Luci looked down at her ice water, the condensation from the glass creating a small pool on the tabletop. She sighed and shook her head.

"And besides, I thought you liked the funeral home. It gave you that sense of morbid curiosity," I said.

"Heat of the moment. I assure you," she said. Even with the triple-digit degree dining room, Luci shivered. "Let's just go visit him. Maybe he knows people like you."

"People like *us*," I corrected. "And I told you we can't. He's dead. My Crew cleaned him up after a drug-fueled party."

The man came back over with our food. He set the salad down in front of me and the corned beef hash in front of Luci. He threw down some silverware and stumbled away, almost knocking down the Casablanca poster again as he yelled at someone in the kitchen.

"But you know, if we can't figure things out, I heard about a place," I offered.

Luci rotated our plates.

"Yeah?" she asked, looking up from her salad.

Her eyes told me to continue. It felt like a bad idea but right then, there *were* no ideas, you see.

"Have you ever heard about the Devil's Alphabet Society?"

Luci scoffed. "An old wives' tale. They would have been outed by now if they actually did exist." The tone in her voice wasn't quite disbelief. I moved my food around on the plate, watching the greasy tracks it created on the porcelain. Luci rolled her eyes at me. "Okay then, hotshot. What about them?"

"They're real. They'd take us in. But we'd have to stay there. Become a part of what they are. What they stand for."

Luci seemed to consider it, assaulting her greens.

"I don't think I'm ready for that kind of life change. This will fade. They will forget about us or maybe we can move to Canada or someplace our faces won't be recognized. We can stay at the funeral home for the time being," she said, stabbing her fork into a cherry tomato. Balsamic ran off the plate and onto the table.

"Fine."

The hash was dry but I was starving. I ate my entire meal in less than five minutes while Luci scooped up her soggy lettuce. The rain stopped.

"Maybe we should try to get to know each other better. Maybe we can learn something that would help us," I offered.

Luci finished the salad and pushed away the plate. A big ring of raw red onion sat in the dressing like an ancient life preserver.

"Give me your cell phone. I need to go outside and make a call," she said.

I grabbed the phone out of my pocket, looked at the scratched-up screen then showed it to her. "No bars. No service in these parts."

She held out her hand instead and said, "Give me the fifty-five cents."

I reached into my other pocket and handed her the change.

"You want to know about me? I have a dog and it needs to be fed and let out. And we obviously can't go back to my place. I'm calling my neighbor to have her take care of it."

That was indeed something I didn't know about her. She got up and walked to the opposite side of the diner to a payphone mounted on the wall. I watched her deposit the coins and dial. A massive flare-up shot out from the kitchen and I heard the server yell again after the flame subsided. Luci watched me as she spoke into the plastic black receiver of the phone.

We were full but we still had no plan, and I still didn't know much about Luci. She knew much more about me. I worked for a Crew, I stole banned books, I had a hideout and a bad habit of trying to save her life. She, apparently, had a dog.

I looked up from my water and saw Luci walking back to the table. She made eye contact with the server, waved her hand for the check, and slid back into the booth.

"What's your dog's name?" I asked.

She looked around, eyes settling on the pastry counter next to the register.

"Muffin."

"What do you do for work?"

"I'm an accountant," she said, keeping an eye out for our server. "Look Mr. Twenty Questions, let's do this back at the funeral home. I'm full and I'm tired and I—"

A salt shaker from the booth behind Luci flew off the table and shattered on the dingy checkered floor. The glass and salt sprayed out like a dry firework. Next, a hand shot out, grasping at a chair from the table adjacent to the booth, knocking it over as well.

Luci and I both looked in the direction of the commotion. A man with a belly that should have prevented him from sitting in a booth, stumbled out from the table. His right hand was still looking for something to grab onto. His left hand groped at this thick neck as he gasped for air, his throat only allowing small gurgling noises.

"Luci, he's choking!" I hissed to my companion. The rest of the diner went on eating their meals, drinking their burnt coffee and paying their checks. We were the only ones looking.

The man tried to cough, his face turning purple, his lips turning blue. Sweat poured down his forehead in sheets. He bumped into a table across from him now, sending it sliding almost ten feet. He twirled around, both hands now at his neck.

I got one foot out of the booth and my butt lifted off the bench seat before Luci reached over and shoved me back down. "No, we are not going to save him," she said, staring into my wandering eyes.

"But what about all that horseshit you fed me about wanting to save people? About helping and healing? About conserving life?" I asked. The man continued his strange dance.

"Now's not the time," she said. "Do you want a repeat of what happened at the pool? And keep your damn voice down."

She was right. Damnit she was right. But what would it matter really? We were already on the run. But perhaps we wouldn't get so lucky this time, if that's what you could even call our current situation.

I sat back down. The choking man was losing energy, losing life. He couldn't keep his eyes open. Both hands fell away from his neck. He swayed on his feet then fell backward, clocking his head on the table he had inadvertently pushed away from him. He hit the ground hard, spread out and ready for a comical chalk outline. Blood coalesced around the wound in the back of his head, spreading into a substantial puddle.

"I'm sure they'll call this one in pretty soon. Jesus," I said looking at the dead man. But then again, with the current state of the restaurant, maybe not.

The fellow in the booth that was with him reached across the table and took the dead man's half-eaten double bacon cheeseburger in both hands and took a giant bite. Grease and burger juices ran down his chin and soaked into his shirt. He took in another mouthful before putting the burger down on his own plate, paying no mind to his newly deceased friend.

The server scooted around the dead man on the floor, being careful not to step in the blood puddle and set the check down on our table. Another fireball burst from the kitchen serving window.

"Godammit! I told you fucks back there to be careful with the grease traps! Christ on a cracker!" the server yelled.

I was starting to think he might be a server and the manager. He took off toward the back again.

I grabbed the check and we headed toward the register to cash out. The rain had started again but was more of a misty patter. Patches of sunlight tried to sneak through the diner's grease-stained windows.

Another burst of flames about took off my eyebrows as I approached the sales counter. A line cook in a mottled smock and black chef's pants burst through the kitchen door, head engulfed in flames. Miraculously, the Ghost Rider look-a-like spun around the coffee bar and into the dining hall without spreading the fire. Globs of the young man's flesh melted off his skull like soft Playdough, plopping onto the tile below. I couldn't tell if the cook was squealing or if the fire was hissing as it devoured the human tinder.

Luci eyed the man in flames as he tripped over the body already on the ground, expired from a bad bite of burger. The two lay together like mismatched socks.

"So does death just follow you wherever you go then?" Luci asked, staring at the dead men.

"No," I answered. "I usually follow death."

# Chapter 11

Some time ago, probably in my early twenties, I got dispatched to the Franklin Zoo on what has still got to be the strangest cleanup I've ever encountered. The story goes like this: A man, his wife and their five-year-old child had taken the day to go see some animals at the zoo since the weather had started to cooperate for doing so. The trouble started at the kangaroo exhibit.

The exhibit was sunken down into the earth guarded against the humans by a rickety three-foot mesh fence that had, up until then, worked just fine at separating the men from the beasts. The child climbed up the barrier and sat on the ledge next to his mother so that daddy could take their photo. What happened next only took a few minutes but was the reason the kangaroo habitat now has twelve-foot walls.

First, the child lost his balance, falling backward into the kangaroo pit. His mother, reflexively, reached out to try to grab the child and ended up falling the ten or so feet down into the enclosure as well. The kid cried, the mom bled and everyone else at the zoo watched the animals. They went on licking their ice cream and taking their photos like normal human beings.

Only one kangaroo had the curiosity to hop over and see what fun new creatures had wandered into its home. The mom stood in front of her child, a protective stance against the roo. The animal kicked her once and she went flying back onto the ground, knocking her own child over. The kangaroo pursued, grabbing the woman by her neck and clawing at her face until it popped one of her eyes like a squishy peeled grape. White runny fluid ran down her scratched and bloodied cheek. The animal let her drop and gave her a final thrusting kick that caved in the left side of her skull.

The child, still crying, sat on the ground frozen in place. The kangaroo picked him up and shoved him headfirst into its marsupium, effectively suffocating the kid. The father, meanwhile, had put his phone back into his pocket and went to go enjoy the exhibit for himself, as many of the other patrons were still doing. Everything was normal. Normal until daddy started to spasm and jerk, his feet climbing the small fence seemingly by themselves. His urges to save and protect overtook his duty to deflect death.

The kangaroo watched him leap into his domain and hopped over to confront him next. The daddy sprinted at the beast and let out a wild scream as he swung a haymaker at the animal, connecting with its smallish head. The kangaroo was stunned. The daddy pulled his son out of the beast's pouch and laid him on the ground shaking the boy to try to get him to wake up.

The kangaroo swung its meaty tail and knocked the father down. But before the animal could do much else, the man popped up and started boxing the beast. Most of the zoo-goers had left at this point to go watch the lion feeding scheduled a few minutes from then. They ended up missing a hell of a show. The man took a few blows but managed to get behind the roo and choke it out. The child started crying again, surviving the black hot mess of the kangaroo's insides, as the father crawled over to cradle him and his dead wife.

Not only was this the strangest cleanup scene I had come across, but it was also the first time I encountered the Retribution Squad who had been dispatched right before us. They scooped up the father and the child, putting them into their black and yellow SUVs. The father more than likely going to prison for life from the stories I'd heard, the son, who by their calculations escaped death, went to go get equalized. That part I knew for sure. A life saved creates chaos. The Retribution Squad is the equalizer and brings everything back into balance.

Outside the funeral home, two of those same black and yellow SUVs, lights ablaze, blocked the entrance to our safe space. *My* safe space. We watched them from behind the decrepit pallets where I normally hid my bike as they went in and out of Lefton's.

"I guess we won't be staying at the funeral home for now, will we, stud bucket?" Luci said.

"I don't understand. No one even knows about this place!"

"Apparently someone does. Don't be so surprised. We are wanted criminals. Our faces are probably plastered all over every local news network. Looks like we're a little fucked."

The Ret Squad officers returned to their SUV with my damn backpack in tow. I couldn't remember if I had removed the stitched in name tag from the inside front pocket but I suppose it didn't matter anyway. People saw me at the pool. Officers almost kicked down my apartment door. They found my safe place and our ugly mugs probably *were* being broadcast over the airwaves. Luci was right; we were a little fucked.

We waited another five minutes, watching the officers talk amongst themselves and their radios. Eventually, the SUV that contained my backpack, all my banned books, took off down the street opposite the pallets we hunkered behind. Lucky us. The remaining SUV stayed behind, probably to see if we would come back.

"I think it's time you reached out to your pals, Ethan," Luci said, eyes still on the Ret Squad. I couldn't tell if she was smiling or not, couldn't think of a reason to, but she looked calm either way. Me on the other hand, oh boy. My heart felt like a jackhammer and it may just as well have been raining again. Sweat saturated my hair.

She was right though; this current little venture was a dead end. There was no going back inside nor recovering my backpack. If we didn't think we were on the run before, well we were now.

I felt the familiar rectangular shape of my phone in my pocket, seeming to burn hot against my thigh, almost as if it too knew what had to happen next. I patted it and looked over to Luci.

"We shouldn't do it here. We need to leave before they see us," I said. "Come on, follow me."

We ended up in an alley between two buildings that used to employ a life insurance company and an abortion clinic. The doors and windows had long since been boarded up, much like the funeral building. We took cover behind a dumpster that still smelled like it may have been full of aborted fetuses. I took out my phone and the piece of paper with the Society's number scratched on it. The battery bar on the phone's home screen indicated that I had a thirteen percent charge left. Good enough for government work.

"Don't just stare at the thing like it's a pair of tits, dial their number," Luci said.

She was truly a poet.

I typed in the phone number and pressed dial. It rang. So far so good. It rang again. And again and again and again. It rang until the automated message told me the person I was dialing did not have a mailbox that was set up and the call ended.

"Well?" Luci asked, craning her face toward me.

"No answer. No way to leave a voicemail."

She closed her eyes and shook her head. I heard the crunch of glass, probably remnants of an old wine bottle, as she paced farther down the alley. A pair of clouds that suspiciously looked like kangaroos hovered over the ancient insurance building.

"Call them back. They'll have to answer eventually," Luci said.

She was probably right, but I didn't want to waste any precious battery I had left. I opened my mouth to say as much but the phone started to vibrate in my hand. I looked down at it.

"It says Unknown Number."

"Well answer it, dummy!" Luci hissed at me.

I did as she bade and answered the call, holding the phone close to my ear.

"Hello?"

Luci looked on with great concertation, her eyes opened wide and her forehead wrinkled up like a Shar-Pei.

"Yes," I answered the voice on the other end, "He thrusts his fists against the posts and still insists he sees the ghosts."

A turkey vulture circled above us, over the dumpster probably waiting for Luci and me to leave. The voice on the other end rattled on for fifteen more seconds and the call ended. Luci put her hands up to each side as if demanding an answer.

"We need to go to Armada Orchards. It's about two hours east of the city. Then we are to park and walk a mile in through the apple trees until we come to a pear tree. It's the only pear tree in the orchard. Then we are to wait there," I told her.

"We will need a car. A: we are not going to go back and get your bike. Too dangerous. And B: I'm not riding on your damn handlebars all the way the fuck out there," she said.

The turkey vulture alit on a window ledge across from the dumpster. I couldn't be sure but it looked like it was drooling.

Can birds drool?

"Yeah, that makes sense. We'll just pop over to the Hertz and get a rental. Maybe a midsize so we can stretch our legs a bit," I said.

Oh boy, she did not appreciate my sarcasm. I do this thing where I get really sarcastic when I'm nervous. I have to admit, it's not very endearing. She moved toward me, I was expecting a blow, but she passed by the dumpster and out of the alley. Naturally, I followed.

Luci looked down the street, her eyes settling on an ancient gold Oldsmobile. She pointed at it and there I was again, following her. She tried the door handle and it was unlocked. The big boat of a car's door squeaked as she opened it. Inside she searched for the keys, flipping down the visors, pulling out the ashtray (yep, there was an actual ashtray, the 1970s were wild) and looking under the seats. I stood by keeping an eye on the empty road, expecting the Retribution Squad to come rolling up any minute.

"Damnit," Luci said under her breath. She got out of the car and went back toward the alley. "Wait here."

She came back holding a good-sized chunk of a broken wine bottle. She got back into the car and started ripping wires out from underneath the steering column. Once the two wires she was after were identified, she took off her shirt and wrapped it around the piece of glass then started to slice through the tangled mess.

Instinctively, I turned away after she had her shirt off. I'm not modest or gentlemanly or anything, but you saw how I reacted in the funeral home while she had me pinned down. I just get a little nervous. I turned back around when I heard her shout a profanity.

"Lift the hood," she said to me as she popped the latch from the car cabin. Again, like a good little puppy, I did as I was told and propped up the massive piece of steel.

"What are we looking for?" I asked.

Luci joined me in front of the car, eyes scanning the engine bay. Then she laughed when her gaze fell upon the car battery.

"Oldest trick in the book," she said. She reached down and grabbed a thick black wire, fitting it to the top of the battery. "Can't start the car if the power isn't hooked up."

I nodded my head in agreement. I knew nothing about cars. I never even got my license, I think I told you that. She could have told me the flux capacitor was burned out and I would have acquiesced all the same.

Once inside the car again, Luci touched the two stripped wires together, creating tiny little sparks. The car made a rumbling noise then quit. She kept at the wires, the sedan making that same noise off and on. It finally roared to life, shaking like a frightened dog.

"Yes!" Luci shouted. Her grin stretched from ear to ear. She looked at the dash. "Half a tank of gas. That should do the trick.

As she was putting her shirt back on, my shirt, I asked, "Where did you learn to hotwire a car like that? Accounting School?"

Still smiling, she said, "You're not the only one that's read a book or too, Ethan. Hop in. Let's fucking go."

I was beginning to think that she wasn't an accountant.

# And Now a Word From the Retribution Squad…

Captain Kiermaier sat at his bulk of a desk sharpening a pencil with a pocket knife. Wood shavings littered the top of the bureau, pieces of the pencil ending up in his lukewarm coffee as well as his inbox. A beat-up black backpack—and by the looks of its heft, full of bricks—slammed down onto the Retribution Squad Captain's desk. The pencil shavings scattered in its wake like startled bugs.

"What the hell is this?" Kiermaier asked, looking up at the detective that deposited the bag.

"Evidence," the detective said. "Take a look inside."

Kiermaier grumbled and set the pencil down. Inside the bag, he saw that it wasn't a load of bricks but a litany of books that were probably just as heavy. He drew one out. It was titled *A Survival Guide for the End of Times* and Kiermaier smiled.

"Lieutenant Gillespie's tip bore fruit. And look at that. Ethan Pointe's name patch is still sewn on the inside of the bag," the detective said.

A metallic tang flowed through the saliva in Kiermaier's mouth. He chortled. He was excited. This was what the job was all about. Retribution. Equalization. Keeping things normal. Fitting in. He put the book back in the bag and handed it again to the detective.

"Where is Ethan and his little accomplice at now?" the captain inquired. He picked up his pencil and resumed his knife work.

"They went to a diner after they fled his apartment and then to an abandoned funeral home. We canvassed each location and came up with this," the detective held up the backpack, "at the funeral home. They should still be in the area. About time to wrap this one up? Bring them in?"

Even though the shades were drawn up in the office, the overhead light worked overtime to illuminate the room. Outside it had been dark and rainy. The sun finally started to peek through but it would be a while still until the clouds moseyed on their way.

"Nope, not yet. This is a 'bigger fish to fry' sort of situation. You'll understand when we get to that point. Ethan is a little bitty fish in a big fucking pond but we have reason to believe he's going to swim us right over to some other fish we've been after for quite a long time. Tell the Ret Squad to pack it in for now and when Lieutenant Gillespie relays more information, that call goes straight to me. Understand?"

The detective nodded his head and hefted the backpack down to the evidence lockers. Kiermaier swiveled around in his chair and inserted the freshly sharpened pencil into a custom-built .50 caliber shell casing. He removed a dull pencil from a pile next to his tailor-made pencil holder and began to whittle at it, smiling so big his false teeth glowed like moonlight.

# Chapter 12

When I was a kid, one group home I was in would pack their station wagon full of their charges, which numbered me plus seven others. We'd road tripped it across state lines to visit, well I suppose you'd call them our group home grandparents. The trips themselves were pretty forgettable; lots of open highways, cornfields and livestock. But on this one trip, a summer storm opened up, pounding the station wagon with sheets upon sheets of rain. It reminded me of being in a car wash except the rain was muddy-brown from the tilled-up fields flanking us.

I remember the rain coming down so ferociously, the windshield wipers on full speed couldn't keep up with the deluge. Visibility was naught. And if that wasn't bad enough, once the rain had finally let up, we realized we had been traveling in the wrong lane for the better part of ten minutes. If it weren't for the sparse traffic on those rural highways, a Cleanup Crew would probably have had to pick arms, legs and eyes balls from the stalks of corn surrounding us. And to think I was that close to never being on a Crew myself. Shucks.

We had left the city, blasting through the back roads on the way to the orchard before a similar type of storm fell upon us. The rain wasn't quite as heavy, nor dirty, but it was enough to make Luci squint through the windshield to keep the old rumbling beast on the road.

The worst part though? The Oldsmobile only had one functioning windshield wiper blade. The other wiper arm was bare, the metal clasp where the wiper should have been arched across the windshield, still trying to perform its duty. On the front glass, an etched curve began to form, the sharp metal of the arm creating a deepening groove. A squealing sound rivaled by a train desperate to stop before bisecting a stranded automobile pierced our ears.

The car radio was an AM band only, and instead of listening to static-filled polka, mariachi music or Radio Disney, we traveled in near silence. Even the intense shrieking from the wiper blade became something of a background noise. I'm not good with awkward silence. Another one of my burgeoning personal qualities, so I tried to strike up a small conversation. What could it hurt?

"You know, when I was a kid my group home never had milk? When we'd have cereal in the morning, we had to use tap water," I said. I guess I was feeling nostalgic about my youth after recounting almost dying on that muddy road trip.

Luci turned toward me and said, "That sounds terrible."

"Yeah, it was pretty disgusting."

"No, I mean living like that. I couldn't imagine being in a place where they'd feed you that way."

Interesting. Maybe Luci had empathy after all.

"And what's even more fucked up is that I still eat my cereal like that. I mean, I can afford milk now for the most part. And I get government assistance, but I still eat my Fruity Pebble's with tap water."

"Okay, *that's* disgusting," Luci said, focusing again on the barely visible road in front of us. The car's speed had dropped down to thirty miles per hour. Looked like Luci's empathy well didn't run all too deep.

We traveled on again in the cascading rain, listening to the rhythmic back and forth of the wipers.

"But I get it, I suppose. That's how you were raised. That's how you grew up," she said.

"Maybe you're right," I said.

"Of course I am. It's a learned behavior."

"Only some things are though. One of my group home fathers used to threaten us with a two-by-four when we stepped out of line, even by an inch. I never got the wood but I witnessed a few kids get pretty bloodied up by him. I couldn't ever imagine doing that to someone," I said.

The rain quit all at once and Luci turned off the wipers. The squealing ceased and my ears buzzed with pleasure from the lack of pain. She bore down on the accelerator, the bald tires causing the car the slide around on the wet road.

"Nope. Instead, you save people," she said. I couldn't tell if there was an edge to her voice or if she was trying to concentrate on keeping the Oldsmobile on the road. "I'm not saying that's an endearing quality. Not by a long shot. Look where it's got us for now, but abuse? Hell, even murder for the wrong reason might be worse than saving people. I don't know."

I checked my phone. My GPS was off so I could conserve the little bit of battery we had left, but I had a map pulled up and was able to look at the road markers and figure out where we were. Based on what I saw, we had maybe twenty more minutes.

"What about you? You seem pretty normal. You work as an accountant. You have a pet and it sounds like a good enough relationship with your neighbors. Probably visit your parents on holidays. I imagine you had an okay childhood."

Luci looked at me but didn't respond. She had both hands on the steering wheel, two and ten, guiding us closer to the orchard. I didn't think she was going to say anything at all but a few minutes later she spoke.

"My childhood was fine. My parents..." she paused, pursing her lips, "well, they were accountants too. I have a brother who I don't ever see, and I might get a phone call from mom and dad on my birthday or Christmas. But that's about it. Oh, we had milk though. Always had milk."

"Accounting must run in your family. What about your brother? He's a numbers person too?" I asked.

"I suppose you could say that. He's all about checks and balances. My family feels our profession is like a civic duty," Luci said.

I had never heard of accounting being equated to something so noble. I must have looked pretty confused because, unprompted, she explained herself.

"The type of accounting I do is more like investigative accounting. Setting wrongs right. Making sure people don't get away with the things that threaten our functional society," she said.

I thought about it and said, "So sort of like the SEC then?"

"Sure," she replied. "Close enough."

"Hmm. It could come in handy when we meet up with The Society. Make sure to tell them all that," I said. Couldn't hurt to add that to our resumes, right?

We reached the orchards ten minutes later and parked on a gravel patch of road opposite a rotting wooden sign. The sign, which appeared to have once been painted with bright greens and clean whites, had faded, weathered from years of neglect. But we were in the right place, for the decaying structure still managed to display the words: Armada Orchards.

Beyond the sign, hundreds of diseased trees littered the swampy field. If at one time they bore apples, those years had passed them decades ago. The squalid trees looked as if they'd blow over in a simple storm. They did, however, weather the tempest that we drove through to get to the orchard. Looks could be deceiving.

"So now we walk, huh?" Luci said, looking through the foliage in front of her.

"Yes. For a mile. Until we find a pear tree," I said. Although, if the pear tree looked anything like these apple trees, we might never locate it.

After looking at the mess in front of us for a while, we started to trek through the wasteland of Armada Orchard. As I suspected, the earth was a mucky mess of dead grass and watery soil. It stuck to my shoes and splashed up my legs, soaking my socks and turning them brown. A few times I stepped into a particularly marshy patch of field and had to fight the ground so that it didn't suck the shoe off my foot.

It took us a bit longer than I expected and we marched on in that golden silence, both of us, I think, focusing on navigating the soupy ground. But soon enough it was there. We both saw it at the same time. A pear tree. It stood out like a coffee table hardcover among a throng of mass-market paperbacks. The tree was thick and sturdy, its fruit just visible through its leafy branches jutting from the solid wood. I had never seen a pear tree before, but I didn't imagine it being as tall as it was. The rest of the orchard had been full of runts.

Luci reached out, jumped up and snatched a pear from a low-hanging branch. She bit into the piece of fruit and its clear juices ran down each corner of her mouth.

"Now what?" she asked, chewing the gritty meat of the pear.

She took another bite then lobbed the half-eaten thing to me. My stomach roiled. I didn't realize how hungry I was. It made sense; we hadn't eaten since earlier in the day at the diner. I took a bite from the section Luci hadn't torn into yet and relished in the sweet nectar of the juicy insides.

"They said to just go to the pear tree and wait. I suppose we wait," I said, swallowing my mouthful.

I finished the fruit, eating all but the core and the stem, and tossed it toward an apple tree. It hit a moss-covered tree trunk and broke into two pieces, ricocheting to the ground. I leaned back against the bark, scanning the orchard for signs of life. Signs of anything that would tell us what to do next. And that's when it hit me. A pear. On the shoulder. It came from the branches above me and when I looked up, I found our sign.

"You weren't followed, were you?" said a voice from high in the tree.

I rubbed my shoulder and stared up at the man. Luci started to walk back toward the sound.

"You didn't have to throw a pear at me," I said. It didn't really hurt but still. Who throws a pear, anyway?

"I tried whispering to you but you didn't respond. I'm sorry," the man said as he climbed down from the branch he was perched on.

For some reason, this whole situation reminded me of one time I got piss drunk in the winter and took a leak into a Douglas Fir. A bird flew out and smacked me in the face. I think I was more surprised there were still birds in the woods with a foot of snow on the ground. Either way, I don't seem to have too much luck with trees.

Luci joined us. She picked up the pear that assailed me and took a bite out of it. With a full mouth, she asked, "So are you with the Society?"

"Yes ma'am," he answered. "My name is Juan. I just had to make sure Ethan and yourself weren't followed by anyone before I could grant you passage to your new home."

After another bite, Luci handed the pear to me. I accepted as our new guide continued.

"I'm sorry ma'am, I don't know your name. They had Ethan up there on the television, picture and all. They just had a stock silhouette and a title of 'female accomplice' for you," Juan said, nodding at Luci.

The sky was slowly starting to darken, driving the humidity to wherever it goes when the moon decides to stir. In another hour, maybe two, it would be hard to navigate the orchard without some sort of light.

"Looks like we're famous, beefcake," Luci said to me. "Well, at least you are buddy boy. And my name is Luci."

Luci extended a hand and Juan shook it. It looked like he grimaced a bit at the grip. I tossed the pear I was eating, wondering again how this tree survived considering its arboreal neighbors.

"So, we have a little way more to walk and then we get to the van to drive the rest of the way to our little compound. Willard will be very glad to see you again. And your friend Luci, too," Juan said and smiled.

He took out a thin burlap sack that was tucked into his waist and opened it up. Great, here comes the ol' cat-piss sack over the head business again.

"But before we leave," Juan began, "I need you to help me gather up as many pears as you can and toss them in this bag. Willard loves pears and always gets a bit miffed if I don't come back with some when I bring in new citizens."

# Chapter 13

I recognized the van the second I saw the interior. The inside was void of seats save for the two up front. It was the same vehicle Willard had abducted me with not long ago.

"Sorry, no air-conditioning in this thing," Juan said, turning to us as we plodded along. "Radio works though."

"Great," Luci said as he turned up the volume. I didn't recognize the song. Something fast-paced with a beat. I suppose it wasn't terrible.

Whatever path we had to take from the orchard to the compound was a bumpy one. Probably not made for cargo vans. Luci leaned forward and thumped my knee once Juan had his eyes back on whatever passed for a road.

"What?" I asked. She put a finger to her lips and shushed me. Juan remained face forward.

"I need your phone," she said.

"Why?"

"So I can call my neighbor about Muffin. Doesn't look like we'll be going back home. Like ever. I need to make sure she'll be taken care of."

"Fine," I said, reaching into my pocket. "Why do you have to be so secretive about it?"

"Use your head, Ethan. A place like this, a people like the Society? They probably don't welcome technology like that. It can track you and potentially give away your location. I just need to use it for thirty seconds and hopefully, they don't confiscate it right when we get there."

She kind of had a point. And I owed her at least that much. I slid the phone to her while Juan still had his back to us. Luci grabbed it and mouthed "thank you".

"Home sweet home," Juan yelled over the radio. In front of us, two iron gates swung open to reveal the compound. Willard appeared from inside a building directly in front of us and waved. Juan parked the van and handed the keys to another man by the iron gate as we all departed the vehicle.

"Ethan, my friend. Welcome," Willard said. He wore that same friendly smile as he had donned on our first encounter. He stuck out his hand and I shook it.

"Willard, this is Luci," I said, nodding to my accomplice.

"The pleasure is mine and I hate to be a bother this soon into introductions, but my back teeth are floating. Do you have a restroom I could use?" Luci asked.

Willard chuckled and said, "I'm sure the journey has been a long one. And it's really no bother. Juan here will show you to the nearest facilities."

Juan led Luci toward another building, next to the one at the entrance. She looked over her shoulder, back at us as she and Juan walked away.

"I'll give you and your friend a more proper tour tomorrow morning when we have a bit more light and the place is more alive, but this is the gist of it," Willard said, spreading his hand across the small village.

Well, small wasn't the right word from what I could see. In the waning light, I couldn't make a proper judgment. At this point, beggars couldn't be choosers and I was happy to be someplace safe.

"We have housing quarters near the back," Willard continued, "where you'll be staying. We grow our own food, for the most part, except on those rare occasions we sneak off into the weird world but that's always a risk. I hope you like pears and sweet potatoes."

Willard led me down the perimeter of the compound and past the gates again. Between the buildings and where the land was more spread out, they had torches set up to provide light. The fire reminded me of the line cook from Mel's. I wondered if he had been cleaned up yet. Probably so.

"I know you guys have been here for a long time, but how have you never been found? I had a little hiding spot I thought of as safe and the Ret Squad found it pretty easy," I said.

My feet were soaked from the trek through the orchard and I was finally realizing how uncomfortable they felt. But alas, the tour continued.

"I'm sure part of it is luck. But since we were granted this land so many decades ago, before The Society was on anyone's radar, we haven't had any visitors. We are a forgotten bunch," Willard said, "for the most part."

A forgotten bunch. A strange term for the living but quite fitting for the dead these days.

"Over there is the solar field. We do have electricity but we try to use it sparingly. Hence the torches. But with it, we still have a link to the outside world and can keep up with current events without being tracked. Which reminds me. Do you have a cellular device?" Willard asked.

I felt my pocket and had a moment of panic when the familiar rectangle shape wasn't there.

"Luci has it," I said.

"As I'm sure you can understand, we cannot allow those devices on the premises. We will need to have it but it will be stored safely if it were to ever be needed again."

I didn't quite know how to take that. Did they kick people out who didn't play by the rules?

"We don't excommunicate folks," Willard said.

This man was a mind reader.

"We will work with you but perhaps one day in the future, those devices may come in handy," he said. "Or maybe not."

As the torch lights faded, we crested a hill and came upon a river flanking the side of the property. Its waters were calm but steady.

"Ah, this is my favorite place," Willard said, smiling at the water. "This is the Thomasville River. As you can see it runs perpendicular to the main gate and walls and acts as a natural barrier. And it's a nice peaceful place to come and think."

From behind us, Juan and Luci made their way up the hill.

"Is this where you get your water?" I asked.

"Luckily, we have a well on site. And yes, we have plumbing. The land might be old but it was also set up for suburban housing shortly after the Orchards were put in. I guess lucky for us the construction didn't pan out," Willard said and chuckled.

The place seemed too good to be true. Considering the circumstances on why I was there, given the choice, I think

I would have signed up to move in regardless. I could always get used to sweet potatoes.

"Welcome back," Willard said, greeting Luci and Juan. "I understand you have a cell phone. Unfortunately, I will need to have it."

Luci handed the phone over.

"Battery is dead," she said.

"No matter. Better that way," Willard said. "I was just giving Ethan a small rundown of the facilities. I'm sure he can fill you in but we will get more in-depth tomorrow. You'll each be assigned a job based on your skills. You'll be fed, housed and clothed and while it might not be what you're used to, I think you will become quite happy here."

"Luci is good with numbers. She's an accountant," I blurted out before she could even open her mouth.

"Wonderful. That will come in handy if we ever get audited on our taxes," Willard said. He winked at Luci.

I'm sure the babbling of the water didn't help but my body started to shut down. It had been a day. I definitely wasn't used to this much excitement between the running, the constant change of plans and, well I guess you could throw in the sex too. If you are so inclined to call it that. I straightened my back, stretched out my arms and yawned, my jaw popping as it unhinged.

"Ah yes. You both must be exhausted. I'll have Juan show you to your quarters so you can get some rest. Come find me when you wake up tomorrow," Willard said. He raised a hand in salute and departed back to the heart of the camp. "Once again, welcome. We are glad to have you here."

Juan led us a different way down the hill, a five-minute walk, toward the back of the property. There we were put into a small room with two beds and a little window. I was already happier about it than my old apartment. Luci poked her head in and sighed. Maybe about the room. Probably about having to share it with me.

"There's a bathroom down the hall on the right if you need it. We will get you some toiletries tomorrow. I'm two buildings over to the east in the first room if you need anything. If not, have a good night," Juan said.

He left and Luci zombie-walked over to one of the beds. I took my shoes and socks off, my feet instantly thanking me.

"If I snore, don't wake me up. Deal with it," Luci said as she fell into bed.

I made my own way into bed, staring up at the dark ceiling thinking about the day's events. My body felt like a train wreck but my mind was racing a thousand miles an hour. I couldn't turn it off. I never could. But I closed my eyes and tried anyway.

"Goodnight, Luci," I said.

Luci was already snoring.

# Chapter 14

The earliest dream I can remember having, I was riding bikes with my friend Darnell. I didn't actually have any friends, but in my dream, I just knew we were pals. We rode up this gravel road and came to a barbeque grill, coals already glowing. Behind it was a giant whale. I couldn't tell you which kind but that sucker was enormous. Darnell and I got off our bikes and started preparing whale steaks. You know, just a couple of six-year-old boys fixing up some southern-style seafood.

I've always had vivid dreams. And most of the time they didn't make any sense. Like when I fell asleep after finally getting used to Luci's snoring. I dreamt that a giant salamander was hunting me. My mind, I think, has a propensity for sci-fi proportioned creatures. Anyway, that big bastard got me cornered in some makeshift hut after chasing me down. And then the silly thing spoke to me. It said 'I'm not trying to kill you' and I said something like 'Well, what the hell you after me for then?' and Mr. Salamander said 'I'm just guiding you' like it was the most natural thing in the world.

Then I started to have one of those moments where you're asleep but you know you're asleep, like I was about to wake up and the reptile said to me 'We're just going to talk, then there's death, but you can do it.' And then I did wake up. It was Luci. She was shaking me.

"Hey, come with me," she said.

"What time is it?" I asked, rubbing the sleep from my eyes.

"I don't know. I don't have a watch. Or a cell phone. But the sun is starting to come up."

And it was. I could see the sky through our little window, fading from a deep purple to an almost white orange. I put on my shoes and followed Luci out of the building.

"Where are we going?" I asked.

"Let's go have a sit down by the river. I just wanted to talk to you but I didn't want to wake anyone up."

There were several more rooms down the hall in the building we slept in. From the sounds of the occupants snoring, they'd get along fine with my partner.

We traversed the same hill Willard had us on last night and went a bit farther to the riverbank and sat down. The morning was pleasant. It would all change once the sun woke up and began roasting the day like a Thanksgiving turkey but right here and now, I couldn't complain.

Luci fidgeted with her hands and stared off into the distance, past the river and into the tree line that flanked the field beyond it. Somewhere over there, birds began their hymns to the rising sun.

"I just wanted to apologize for the way I have been acting. The way I have been treating you. You've only been trying to help, and I see that but I'm stressed out, tired and not sure what the hell is going on anymore," she said.

"You don't owe me an apology," I responded, picking up a small stone and tossing it into the river.

"I owe you my life," she said.

I suppose that was true enough. But also, I knew I made her life much more complicated considering the past twenty-four hours or so.

"And I understand that I won't ever have that same kind of life before I met you. I think that's why I've been such a bitch. But still, I appreciate the fact that I even have a chance to live and while it might take some time to get used to this place, I'm grateful for you and all that you've done to help me."

Getting a read on Luci, for the short amount of time that I knew her, well it was like trying to stick a wet noodle up a cat's ass. Not easy. But maybe it was because she was traveling through the stages of grief, you know? Shock and denial: the broken bottle to her neck in my apartment. Or maybe that was the pain and guilt? I'm sure Willard had a book on all this.

"And I'm not good at this whole talking about my feelings crap so don't go thinking I want to hear any of yours. It's just that I needed to say this, get it off my chest because you must feel like I hate you. But I don't. Not really."

Anger and bargaining: is it possible that these might be passive attributes of Luci's ego even before fate intertwined us? Yeah, probably.

'So, thank you for just listening and not trying to relate your experience to seem like I have it made or something."

Depression and loneliness: that was obviously the sex at Lefton's Funeral home.

"But like I said. We are here now, we're safe and we have a new purpose."

The upward turn: looking at a directory, this would be the "You are here" moment.

Luci stayed quiet after that. I didn't want to fuck anything up by talking so we both sat there and listened to the birdsong. Soon enough there would be reconstruction and working through and the chance at having hope and acceptance.

What a difference a day can make.

The sun was rising, the air was calm and Luci didn't hate me. Things actually started to look better for me. For us.

That's when the shouting started.

It came from behind us, over the hill and toward the front gate. From where we sat, the noises were incomprehensible but clearly amplified as though orders were being barked through a loudspeaker.

Luci and I turned toward the commotion. The hill blocked our view of what was happening so we Army crawled up the incline to get a better look. My eyes crested the hill and what I saw shouldn't have shocked me but I began to tremble anyway. My skin turned cold in the rising humidity. Even from a hundred yards away, I recognized the source of the shouts. I recognized the uniforms with the black and yellow bands around the chest area. The Ret Squad had arrived.

"Holy shit fuck. They found us. They followed us and found us," I whispered to Luci even though there was a snowball's chance in hell that anyone would hear us.

"Shut up. You don't know that. They might have been casing this place for days. Maybe weeks," she said.

There must have been two dozen of them, armed with their rifles pointed at the main building by the entrance. The building with all of the compound's resources and books and what little technology we had linking us to the outside world.

Willard came out from the building and stood before the Ret Squad. More amplified voices. I couldn't tell from here but Willard seemed to be engaging them, communicating with his hands. In one of those hands, it looked like he grasped some sort of remote control. The rifles swung and pointed directly at him.

"What are they doing?" I asked Luci. She continued to stare on.

By now several members of the commune had woken up and shuffled out to investigate the commotion for themselves. They didn't venture too close to the scene but the Ret Squad still took notice and a handful of the militia shifted their concentration—and rifles—from Willard to the compound residents.

"What should we do? Should we go down there and try to help him?" I asked.

"Help him with what? We're safe behind the hill for now. Just shut up and let's see what happens." Luci responded.

More shouting. It looked like a standoff.

"What the hell are they doing?" I asked again.

Willard backed himself into the building from whence he came, and slowly, two members of the Ret Squad paced after him. All three of the group disappeared into the structure. My body started to sweat like I was back in my apartment after a long day of cleaning up bodies.

Were they in some sort of weird negotiation now? Discussing terms of surrender? A minute later, things turned from the tranquil possibility of an Appomattox

Court House to the blazing trails of a burning Atlanta in the aftermath of Major General William Tecumseh Sherman. I didn't do great in school—imagine that—but for some reason, the Civil War seemed to stick with me.

The explosion shook the ground beneath me. I felt a hot wave of air flash against my face as I watched the book building burst into debris and flame. Startled screams on both sides of the conflict followed.

"The fuck just happened?" Luci said.

I didn't have to answer. I think she knew as well as I did what just happened. And as if to answer the question, a flaming forearm, once attached to someone in the building, soared through the air and landed about twenty yards in front of the hill. Smoke rose from the flaming fingers in tendrils. It didn't smell too differently from a barbeque.

There was no stopping it. The acid rose from the pit of my empty stomach and I felt the warm fluid travel through my throat before it evacuated my mouth, covering the lush grass. The shouting started up again, no loudspeaker this time, and the report of machine-gun fire echoed through the compound. I closed my eyes and slid back down the hill. Luci remained where she was until I started to sit up again.

"Get down, Ethan! Don't let them see you!"

Luci slid in next to me and pulled me down. We were both on our bellies facing the river now. She could have dragged me out to that river and drowned me like she was supposed to have been at Dowding such a short—and long—time ago. I probably would have let her. My mind was in shock. I moved without thinking. Willard was dead. The dream was dead.

"They're going to kill us," I said. The words slurred as they escaped my mouth.

"Listen to me," Luci said, grabbing me by the shoulders. "See those trees on the other side of the water? We are going to ford the river and sneak in behind those trees and follow the field back to the front of the orchard. They won't see us. And with any luck, our car will still be there."

The shots ceased but the screaming continued.

"Yes. Yes, all right," I said.

We trudged through the muddy bank and into the slow-moving tepid water. Luci made sure to keep us down from sight of the Ret Squad but truth be told I don't think they'd have seen us from where they were anyway.

The water was shallow. Silver lining. It got as far up as my knees at its deepest. I held Luci's hand for balance. My legs were like trying to walk on two rubber chickens.

"This is stupid. This whole thing is stupid. I miss my apartment, my job. I didn't know how made I had it. I let my stupid mind trick me into thinking life was meant to be anything else than what it is. I shouldn't have taken those books from Wallace. I wish I never had," I said, pausing before the next sentence spilled from my lips.

"I wish I would have never saved you."

I was a few short breaths away from hyperventilating and nary a paper bag was in sight.

"Well, that's your own damn fault. I never asked you to. And we are here now so suck it up and get behind these trees so we can get the hell out of here," Luci said.

The tree branches scraped against my ashen skin as if they were trying to grab me, pull me in and tell me their secrets. The smoke from the explosion continued to rise into the sky like a beacon. Luci put her hand on my back and forced me through the rest of the scrub and to the field behind the trees.

"Stay moving," she said, pointing toward the direction of the front of the orchard.

"The car. We can't use the car. That must be how they found us. They knew we stole it and used it to get here. They followed us because of the car!" I yelled. My limbs shook like earthquakes.

Luci slapped me, hard, across the face.

"Calm down. Get ahold of yourself. I highly doubt that they followed us. What do you want to do? Take the ankle express to our next destination?"

"But they had to have seen the car when they went through the orchard. They had to have seen it parked off to the side!"

We had walked far enough away to still see the smoke but the voices no longer traveled to our ears. Luci sighed.

"Fine. If the car is even still there, and if the place isn't crawling with more Ret Squad soldiers, we'll dump the damned thing as soon as we can get another one. Deal?"

All I heard was a perfect storm of "ifs".

"And where the hell are we going to go? My face is all over the news and they'll figure you out eventually."

"We'll talk about it in the car if we can get to it. But in the meantime, if you don't shut up, I might just leave you behind," she said.

Knowing what I know now, I should have stayed behind anyway.

# And Now for More Action From the Ret Squad…

The detective opened Captain Kiermaier's door and leaned against the frame. Kiermaier looked up at the intrusion and set down his pad of paper and pen. Reaching into his bag, the detective procured a pear and tossed it to his boss.

"What's this?" Kiermaier asked, catching the fruit.

"That," the detective explained, "is the good news."

Kiermaier surveyed the produce. "It's a pear."

"Not just any pear. That pear comes from the only fruiting tree in all of Armada Orchards," the detective said.

The building's antiquated air conditioning system kicked on, rattling the ceiling tiles as the detective sat down in front of the desk. He retrieved another pear from his bag, wiped it on his shirt and took a bite out of the ripe fruit.

"So then, Gillespie's information was correct once again. About the Orchard. The compound," Kiermaier said. His desk phone began to ring but he silenced the call.

"I guess you could say the lead bore fruit," the detective said as he swallowed his second bite. A dumb smile formed on his lips but the boss narrowed his eyes at the comment.

Clearing his throat, the detective continued. "We executed a raid at 0600 hours this morning, just as planned."

From somewhere down the hall, the smell of burnt coffee wafted its way into the tiny office. The acrid aroma of over-roasted beans seared into Kiermaier's nostrils.

"So, this," he said, holding up his pear, "is the good news. That usually means there's bad news to go along with it."

The detective slunk down into a chair and pushed a long breath through his teeth.

"We infiltrated the compound through the front gate and set up a small perimeter. The first building upon entering the estate is where they kept their contraband and other miscellanies, according to Gillespie's info. The man himself, Willard O'Malley came forth from the building after hearing our Squad leader's commands through a bullhorn. He had in his hand a device he claimed was a detonator remote for various explosive devices throughout the compound and if we didn't leave, he would start setting them off as our soldiers approached.

"O'Malley then backed his way into the building again as Squad members Borneo and Tillman pursued. The three of them were only in the building for around a minute before it blew. We called his bluff and lost. The whole building was destroyed along with O'Malley, Borneo and Tillman. Along with any evidence of contraband."

Kiermaier Nodded.

"Was anyone else injured?"

Now the detective nodded.

"Three more of our team suffered shrapnel and nail wounds but will survive. Apparently, O'Malley had constructed pipe bombs and placed them in the front building and along the perimeter walls. Some real Freedom Club bullshit. Lucky for us, the rest of the devices failed to detonate."

Kiermaier twirled his fingers at his subordinate, signaling for him to go on.

"By this time, members of the society had started to file out from beyond the explosion, most likely woken up by the noise. We did have an incident where a Squad member opened fire on several Society members, killing three, claiming they also had remotes in their hands but none were recovered. That Squad member has been placed on administrative leave and we ended the morning by rounding up dozen or so subjects, all on their way to processing as we speak."

Kiermaier looked at his pear again and smiled, his big white chicklets gleaning in the fluorescents. He began to chuckle. The chuckle transitioned into a full-on laughing spell. The detective joined in as one does when they might not know what the humor in the situation is but gets drawn in by the comedy of it all.

"Well," Kiermaier said, wiping a tear from the corner of his eye, "I always thought there'd be more citizens at the compound. And I would have liked to meet the man. O'Malley. What a brain to pick that would have been. It seems like we've both been at it for so long, me on the righteous side of the law and Willard nowhere near it, perpetuating his evil and nonsense. I've dreamt of this day for so damn long. And all of it has been worth it. We won. By God, we fucking won!"

The detective looked up from his own pear and jumped in his seat as Kiermaier pounded his fists on his desk. A string of saliva hung from his mouth. His eyes were burning with madness, turning his cool blue irises into hardened gray steel. And then, a second later, Kiermaier sat back in his chair, relaxed his jaw and shoulders and looked like the normal Captain that had perched at that desk for some thirty years.

"Of course, reach out to the families of the fallen and get them all squared away. Their sacrifice at the compound was for the greater good and will always be remembered. Now, what about Ethan and his lovely lady friend? Where are we at with them?"

The detective, still frozen after his boss's display of unnatural enthusiasm, cleared his throat and replied.

"They are headed north. It's only a matter of hours before we will take them in. We wanted to make sure everything at the compound was tended to and taken care of first. Gillespie will initiate the retribution sequence with Ethan after he's apprehended."

"Get a hold of Sargent Darnold and have him meet Gillespie there," Kiermaier said.

"Gillespie's not going to like that, boss," the detective said.

"I do not care. Gillespie might not need the assistance but I want Darnold there to make sure this gets done properly. No Funny business. Gillespie has been very close to this situation," Kiermaier said.

The detective stood up and shuffled toward the door.

"Yes sir, I'll get with Darnold right now," he said, pausing at the exit. "Congratulations, sir. I'm proud to be part of this team."

The detective left. Kiermaier stood up from his chair, walked over and locked his office door. He drew the window blinds shut then sauntered back to his desk. From his pants pocket, he removed a set of keys, one of which unlocked the bottom right drawer of his desk. From the drawer, he removed a pristine copy of Playboy's September 1979 issue, a small squeezable tube of hand lotion and a travel pack of tissues. He set the items on his desk before him.

Cracking his knuckles and picking up the lotion, Kiermaier said, "I fucking deserve this."

# Chapter 15

I had to be about twelve years old or so when this story happened. This story I'm about to tell you. It was a semi-rare occasion when I and some of my foster siblings got dropped off at another family's house as a kind of like a play date. But it wasn't so much that it was a play date but a "break" for my foster parents to be childless for a few hours so they could do whatever it is they did with their free time. Probably fuck.

But this one visit stuck out to me more than the others. You see, all the foster parents did this, although sparingly. It was kind of like a rotating occasional babysitting ring but each place we went to was pretty much the same old song and dance. And on this particular occasion, as was par for the course, we spent the entire playdate outside drinking hose water and dreaming of hotdogs because when you went to another foster home to give your own foster parents a "break", you were never fed.

Anyway, after we got picked up by our glowing and recharged guardians, we set upon the path back to our own home (ha, what a misnomer) but dammit I was hungry. And so were Terrance and Bethany, my foster siblings. We knew better, should have known better but when your stomach commands your mind all bets are off the table. Ladies and gentlemen, no more bets, please.

I spoke up first and spoke the loudest. I asked if we could stop and grab some cheeseburgers on the way home. I didn't mind where from. Something cheap. No, sorry, something *affordable*. And because I spoke the loudest, I got hit the hardest. My foster mom—without even turning her neck—slapped the side of my head so hard, my noggin bounced off Terrance.

It all happened in an instant, my body made up its mind before my mind made up its mind. Next thing I know is we are at a stoplight and my seatbelt is unbuckled and I'm climbing over Terrance and I'm opening the car door and I'm rolling out onto the pavement.

And then I started walking. I was going to walk home. From the car, I can hear my foster mom yelling something about how they ain't white trash and they ain't going to follow me and beg me to get back in the car. And she was right. The car took off and I was by myself.

My stomach was rumbling again and I didn't have any funds to procure a burger so I decided to start heading home. Where was I? Not a clue, but I saw a blue road sign pointing to the interstate and I knew the exit off of which I lived. And home was only like a twenty-minute hike once I got off that exit so I decided that's where I'd go.

I won't bore you with how long the damn walk took (four hours) or how many miles I probably walked (thirteen or so) or that at one point as I was walking the shoulder of the interstate, a car slowed down and yelled out the name Mike and pulled over (hey I could be a Mike) and when I jogged up to it, the bastard took off speeding down the interstate again. No, I won't bore you with that stuff. But I did eventually make it home, a little after nightfall and when I tried to open the front door, it was locked. And all the other doors were locked too.

I spent the night outside, curled up underneath the front porch crawl space. The family car was parked in its usual spot in the gravel driveway and it stared at me all night, laughing.

And you know what?

The car was still there.

Not the family car in the driveway but the ugly gold jalopy that Luci hot-wired to get us to the compound. It was still there, tucked away in the corner of what used to be the orchard's parking lot, and I just thought to myself, well at least I won't have to walk from here to wherever we were headed next.

"Hey, earth to Ethan. You want to get the hell out of here or are you just going to stand there with your dick in your hand?"

I turned and looked at Luci, shaking the poltergeist of the memory about my long walk.

"I...I just, yeah, let's go"

And as she had done before, Luci grabbed the wires from under the dashboard, rubbed them together and got us back on the road.

"Where are we going?" I asked, staring out the front window as the countryside passed us by. Trees. Dead grass. Emaciated bovine.

"North. We're going to find another ride and head north."

"What's north?"

Luci clicked her teeth and looked into the rearview. We were the only ones on the road. Good. No Ret Squad.

"My parents have a small two-room cabin, maybe three hours from here outside the Savoy Forest. They use it for camping and getting out of the city when the weather is cooler. It'll be empty right now."

A cabin. Another "safe space" maybe. Instead of relaying this information earlier, we go to the compound and get people killed.

"Don't look at me like that," Luci said, keeping her peepers on the road ahead of us. I didn't realize I had turned to her. I didn't realize I was trying to burn holes through her skull with my eyes. "You had no problem with being at the compound. We had resources there. People to talk to that have been living this life on the run for years. The only thing we'll have at the cabin is shelter and hopefully running water."

I never had an issue with admitting that I was wrong. But Luci just brings out the best in me. I wasn't going to let her know but she *was* right. The compound could have been where I lived and died. Growing food, reading, helping people. That could have been my life until the shit-kicking Ret Squad showed up.

"They're just going to find us again. They found my apartment. They found the funeral home and the compound. Wherever we go, they'll just find us. I'm just going to turn myself in the next place we stop."

I wasn't going to turn myself in. I was just feeling sorry for myself.

"Quit feeling sorry for yourself. They won't find us. You don't have your phone anymore. They were following your location using the pings off the cell towers. Had to have been."

I hated that she was the voice of reason. I hated that she was so damn calm. Somebody's arm, probably Willard O'Malley's, almost landed on top of my head and here Luci is, just driving us to safety. Boy, I could get in a mood sometimes.

Finally, after about thirty minutes of silence between us, we passed a road sign announcing the Township of Elkhorn a few miles ahead. Luci pointed at it.

"We'll get off here to ditch this piece of crap. I'll find us something else, maybe find us some food too. You'll feel better," Luci said.

The town we pulled into, this Elkhorn, was one of those towns that only exist because it's off of a highway exit. There were a few houses on the south side of the main drag where a bank, a pharmacy and a few restaurants stretched on into the nothingness beyond it. This was also one of those towns that people don't actually inhabit. The neighborhood Luci pulled the car into was suspect at best.

From where we were parked, we were in front of a row of dilapidated homes, but I could see the backlot of a Waffle Palace and its connecting property, a grease monkey shop called Dexter's Garage in the opposite direction. Dexter didn't look like he had much business these days but the Waffle Palace seemed to be doing fine.

"I'm going to walk across the street to that waffle joint and see if there are any potential rides for us. I don't see any cameras in the back of the building but just in case, I'm leaving the car here and you are going to stay with it," Luci said.

I nodded and watched her get out and walk across the street then closed my eyes and slid down the passenger seat. Now that we weren't wheels spinning on the pavement, the air became still in the cab of the car. Even with the windows down, I could feel the heat baking into my skin. The wind that cooled us off while on the road was now a ghost gone to visit someone else. An odor that I realized was actually me, made my nostrils burn like small smokey fires.

After a few more seconds of trying to control my retching, I stole a glance out from the car and Luci had made it to the Waffle Palace back parking lot. The first car she sidled up to was a black SUV. She tried the handle and all she could do was jiggle it. Locked. The sedan next to it yielded the same results. Then Luci started to feel up and around the wheel wells but all it did was turn her hands black.

Next to the sedan was another one, a maroon Buick. Luci started to walk over to it when the back door of the Waffle Palace flung open. A heavyset man dressed in a grease-stained apron and hairnet emerged, carrying a white plastic trash bag in his right hand. Luci heard the bang of the door and ducked between the two cars she was casing, out of sight from the line cook. The man walked ten feet to the corner where an open dumpster waited for him to feed it.

Luci felt around the wheel well of the Buick as she crouched and pulled something out from above the tire. I couldn't see what it was. Mr. Line Cook deposited his trash, wiping his sweaty paws on the yellowed shirt beneath his apron, and disappeared back inside the restaurant.

And just like that, we were within inches of being outed but like some sort of female Houdini, Luci escaped again.

Just then, a high wind swept over my sweat-mottled face. It didn't cool me off or anything but at least it helped to carry the stink away from me.

I heard a door open again and my skin turned cold, who needed the breeze? Fear is like ice. But alas, it was Luci opening the door to the Buick. Then she left the vehicle, creeping toward the dumpster, her gait like a child playing hopscotch where every other numbered box was lava.

*What was she doing? Get in the car, Luci. Get in the damned car!*

My lips were dry and my tongue flicked over their moon-like surface as I watched Luci pull the white trash bag from the dumpster. She scampered back to the Buick, jumped inside and closed the door. The engine turned over and the car was alive. I shook my head and couldn't help but smile a bit. This woman never ceased to amaze. She really missed her calling, what with being an accountant and all.

As Luci pulled the Buick out of the parking lot, the back door to the Waffle Palace shot open again. This time it was a taller, lanky man in a black and yellow polo. He walked over to the edge of the building and lit up a cigarette, none the wiser about the grand theft occurring a second before.

I exited the old car as Luci pulled up, happy to be out of the oven of a vehicle and ran over to the Buick's passenger door. The door wasn't as heavy as the gold gremlin we were leaving behind but it still felt like pulling open a bank vault. These seats were cloth, thank you Jesus, and once my door was shut, Luci pointed us back toward the highway and onto the path of the cabin.

There was a key in the ignition. She didn't hotwire this one. I pointed at it and said, "How'd you get the damn keys?"

Luci reached between her legs and grabbed something then tossed it to me. It was a small rectangular tin. On the top, a white key outline was stamped onto the black surface. I thumbed it back and the metal slid open to reveal a small recessed area. In it, another key rattled around. A key with an oval end.

"Flip it over," Luci said.

I did. There was a magnet covering the back.

"I don't get it," I said.

"Don't feel too bad, lover boy. Not many people would. It's a spare key holder. The magnet on the back allows it to adhere to the metal under the wheel well or maybe the frame somewhere on the car. It was something a lot of people did back in the 1980s," she said.

I took the other key out and held it up to my face. A flat piece of metal. No fob. Almost like a house key. I asked Luci if that was what this second key was. She laughed.

"That's the key to unlock the vehicle. The one in the ignition is the one to start it. It looks like that key but it's square on the end instead of round."

Hot-wiring a car? I could never. Figuring out that this car needed two keys to use it? That one would probably take me a while. The 80s were wild.

From the back seat, Luci grabbed the white trash bag she raided from the Waffle Palace's dumpster.

"Here," she said, handing me the bag as she drove. "It was the freshest bag of the lot. I'm sure there's something in there that's edible."

My stomach rumbled at the smell as I untied the bag. The waterfall inside my mouth started to ooze from the corners of my lips. My hunger, perhaps kept at bay with all the anxiety and turmoil of the morning so far, erupted once the bag was open.

"If you find hash browns, I call dibs," Luci said.

The contents of the garbage bag were these: two empty orange juice containers, one half-eaten waffle smeared with coffee grounds, a handful of used coffee creamer vessels, what looked like a whole roll of paper towels, unraveled and wadded up near the bottom of the bag and three Styrofoam containers.

I removed the first of the to-go boxes and an over-easy egg slid off the top, falling to the floor. The yoke exploded at my feet like someone's head striking the concrete after a swan dive off of a tall building. Inside, a plain waffle, two sausage links and a pile of home fries sat, unmolested. I offered the to-go box to Luci and she scooped out the fried potatoes.

"Thanks, now eat up. You're going to need the energy," she said through a mouthful of spuds.

I should have asked her, energy for what? A car ride to safety? A conversation about the benefits of a big breakfast? I'm not sure she would have answered me, and maybe if she did, it would just be another one of her flick of the wrist vague answers, so instead, I did what I was told and stuffed the dry waffle into my mouth. I was used to doing what I was told. I want to fit in. I want to be normal.

# Chapter 16

Between exhausted and wired. That's where I was as Luci drove the car toward our next destination. My vision blurred then focused, like a camera trying to frame a shot. At one point I thought I spotted a police cruiser on the side of the road hiding behind a ground-level billboard. But I blinked my eyes and it was gone. My belly was full but my nerves were shot. Has your head ever throbbed so bad that you could see the color of blood every time it pulsed?

These two days on the run felt like two weeks, but leaving Dowding pool on my bike with Luci in tow seemed like mere hours ago. And I didn't even remember being at the diner until I smelled the garbage bag full of discarded breakfast foods. Two days. Unraveled in two days.

"Can you stop that? It's distracting," Luci said from the driver's seat.

*Was she talking to me?* Of course, she was talking to you, dummy. You're the only other one in the car, right? *Right?*

A gasoline tanker blew by us in the other lane like a chrome demon on wheels. I ducked my head, habit now when we had some rare road company, to hide my face and I saw what Luci was talking about. My foot jackhammered away at the floorboard of the Buick, that wired energy controlling my body. Luci reached over and grabbed my upper thigh to stop my tapping.

"Sorry," I whispered.

Luci released her claw-like grasp but the pain from her grip calmed me down or at least brought me to the here and now. Still, I needed something to distract me until we stopped. Otherwise, I was apt to not only wear on Luci's patience but also wear a hole in the floor mat. So, I decided to strike up a little conversation, my co-conspirator's favorite thing in the whole wide world.

"How long have your parents owned the cabin?" I asked.

Luci grunted and sucked her teeth. She shrugged her shoulders and said, "I don't know. For as long as I can remember."

"Do they have any animals there? Like a goat or some horses?"

"It's a cabin, not a barn. And besides, there isn't always someone there. Animals wouldn't make sense."

Luci pushed up the sunglasses on her face and rubbed her eyes. She found the shades in the glove box after she asked me to see if there was maybe a handgun or a knife. There was not. There were sunglasses and fast-food napkins.

"Yeah, I guess that was a pretty stupid question. It would be nice to see a horse in real life though," I said. It could be my service animal. My emotional support horse. I would ride it around the cabin grounds and train it to kick people who wandered onto the property.

Another vehicle passed us, a pulp truck, and I ducked again.

"How much longer do you think?" I asked.

"Maybe another hour."

Ten minutes passed and I didn't say anything. Conversations with myself were easier to maintain than whatever passed for dialog with Luci. My knee threatened to start running in place again. My skin felt stretched over my body, too tight and too slicked with sweat. Cold, sour sweat. I was running out of material and my delusions started to overtake my mind again.

"Maybe another ten hours," I heard Luci say. She looked over at me and was smiling. The corners of her mouth touched her ears and then she began to laugh. It sounded like a chainsaw. Her sunglasses melted into her face and became her eyes. Black eyes as big as rotting peaches. Skinny gray worms crawled out of the folds of her hair, protruding from her scalp in wiggling waves.

I squeezed my eyes shut so hard I started seeing the veins in the back of my eyelids. *Breathe, Ethan.* I shook my head and opened my eyes.

The pavement stretched on before us. Luci was Luci again, hands on the wheel, eyes on the road. Likely Luci. My mind wasn't playing tricks on me. It was trying to tell me something. To warn me.

*Just keep talking. Get out of your own head.*

My mouth felt like someone had forced me to suck on a restroom hand dryer. I smacked my sandpaper tongue against my papyrus lips and tried to talk.

"You'll miss Muffin, right? Your, what? Your cat, was it?" I asked.

"Sure," she said. "Cats are self-sufficient. My neighbor won't have any problems."

I put my fingers to my nose and breathed in the sticky syrup from my dumpster breakfast and it brought me once again to the diner. Luci gets up. She goes to the pay phone. She talks and hangs up. She sits back down and says she was checking on her…dog. Muffin was a dog. Not a fucking cat.

All right, all right. What else did I know about Luci? What else, what else? She can't swim well. Okay. She snores. Check. Shit. Why couldn't I ever get her to open up? She eats salad. Her parents are accountants. *Bingo.*

"Do your parents keep books at the cabin?" I asked. "I never did finish Catch-22. But maybe it's better that way."

"Never read that one," Luci replied.

Both sides of the road grew thick with trees as we pressed on. The elevation raised and the pavement began to be flanked by ditches leading into the foliage. We were getting closer to the forest. To the cabin.

"Well, I mean professors would keep books at their cabin. Just seems like common sense," I said. My body remained forward in the passenger seat but I glanced toward Luci to see if the professor's title raised any eyebrows.

"They probably have books. I know they have a bed and that's where I'm headed first," she said.

Nothing.

No calling me out.

No backtracking to match the story.

In a flash, my body turned hot. I felt the stinging of needles prickling my face and body. She was lying about her animal. She lied about her parents' professions or at the very least didn't dispute my claim about them. Did she even have a pet? Who would she have been talking to at the diner?

"I need to use the bathroom. Can we stop at the next exit please?" I asked.

Ol' Luci began drumming on the steering wheel with her hands. She yells at me for my restless leg and here she is doing her best John Bonham impression.

"No can do, buckaroo. No gas stations or rest stops between here and the cabin. We'll be there in another half hour. Cross your legs or something," she said.

The bathroom trick didn't work.

"You can just pull over up ahead and I'll go behind that tree," I said pointing to a dip in the terrain ahead.

The car started to slow down, but only because the speed limit dropped. Luci ignored me and kept driving. I didn't know if she was part of this whole Ret Squad mess or if she was just messing with me this entire time but my brain had already decided she was the enemy. If I wanted to be free of her company, I was short on options.

Before I knew what I was doing I grabbed the chrome door handle and pulled. I thought back to saving Luci at the pool and how I swam to her without thinking about that either, before the door inched open against the wind. I pushed it forward enough to slip my arm through the opening and with my left hand, freed myself of the seatbelt.

"What are you—nooo!" Luci must have heard the noise from the wind drag on the door as I pushed it open. She turned to see me tuck and let go of the seatbelt.

We met each other's eyes, or rather my eyes met her sunglasses, as I fell from the moving car. A second later she was gone and the world had turned into an industrial laundromat dryer.

# Chapter 17

Every summer from about the time I was ten to maybe thirteen, me and the neighborhood kids would spend our days playing out in the woods. We'd build forts from the junk we found left there from illegal dumping. One kid had a hatchet he used to chop down branches for imaginary fires and the first summer we even built a latrine. But, between near triple-digit heat and the odorous waste that came out of our bodies, that particular project proved to be a dud.

The biggest constant, however, from my time spent out in those woods was my inability to recognize poison ivy. It knew *me* well though. It never failed, I'd come home and the next day my skin would be all red and splotchy, starting to itch. Then a few days later the rash bumps formed and if you ever had poison ivy like I did, you knew what came next: big bubbles of pus, stretching the skin tight, begging to be scratched. Then they'd pop and the ivy ooze would drip down my arms or legs or chest and infect the rest of my clean skin.

Next came the trip to the doctor—my guardian cursing at me the whole way there—to get a needle of penicillin jabbed in my ass and a boric acid solution to bring home and put on my wounds. The next week or so would be miserable. The itching was insatiable and I cried myself to sleep when the agony started to take precedence over the itch. That was the worst pain I had ever felt in my life.

Until now.

Every bone in my body felt like it had been put in a mortar and pestle. I was upright, sitting against a tree that broke the rest of my fall down into the ditch. I blinked my eyes to try to clear my head and all I could see from the left socket was a filter of red. A blanket of blood gushed out of the laceration on my forehead. That explained my headache.

"What the fuck is wrong with you?"

I recognized Luci's voice without having to look back up to the road. She started screaming something else but my attention redirected to my left leg. A medium-sized branch, sort of like the ones the kid with the hatchet chopped down for us in the summers of my youth, protruded from my quadriceps. I closed my left eye but still saw a blooming patch of darkened red spreading around the intrusion. This was not how I pictured my escape going. But then again, what had gone right up to this point anyway?

"Don't you dare," Luci said and smacked my hand away from the tree limb piercing my leg. Although the woodsy part of where I landed was devoid of any real sound, I still didn't hear Luci come upon me. "You pull that thing out and you'll bleed to death."

The copper taste in my mouth made me thirsty. I wiggled my tongue around to make sure I hadn't bitten it off.

"Oh, you'd like that though, wouldn't you?" I said and spat out a glob of mucus and blood. It ended up in my lap.

"What the hell are you talking about?"

"Don't act stupid. You're one of them. One of the Ret Squaders. You can't even keep your stories straight. Which is it, a cat or a dog? Are you an accountant like your parents? Oh, that's right. They're teachers!"

I tried to raise my hand to flip her off, you know, really make a point, but I couldn't get my arm up more than a few inches before white-hot stabs of pain attacked my shoulder.

"So that's what you think, huh?" Luci said standing up. Her knees popped as she rose.

"Screw you."

"No, screw you, Ethan. Has it ever occurred to you that I've suffered trauma too? I didn't ask for you to save me. I didn't ask to leave my life as I knew it to run around with some thankless fuck who thinks I'm out to get him. Muffin is a dog. My neighbor has a cat and the two of them are like Bonnie and Clyde. I had her cat on my mind, ok? And I never said my parents were teachers or professors or whatever. I was focused on the road, not exactly paying attention to you, for Christ's sake. Not everyone is out to get you. Who are you? You're nobody!"

"Just get it over with. Just kill me," I said. I was a prince at feeling bad for myself. I guess no one else ever really did.

Another vehicle passed by the parked Buick above us. I couldn't see it but I heard it. The wind from whatever it was rustled the unkept highway grass on the shoulder. Luci turned and looked up to the road.

"You're an idiot. If I worked with anyone trying to come after you, I could have let them take you in your apartment. At the funeral home, after we came back from the diner, all I had to do was scream and their guns would have been trained on us. Maybe at the compound, I could have marched you right to the front gates when the Ret Squad announced themselves. And do you really think it's procedure or policy to have sex with the person you're supposedly trying to apprehend?"

She made good points.

Damnit, she made good points. My mind was messing with me ever since we escaped the compound. I don't know if it was PTSD or not but I couldn't think straight. I couldn't see clearly, never mind the sticky sheet of blood covering my eye. And now instead of nearing the cabin where I could have rested my body and my brain, I was broken and helpless.

"Luci look…I'm sorr—"

"You know what? No. Fuck this. I'm out of here. I'm better off without you," she said then started back up the hill toward the Buick. Little pieces of pine needles and dirt rolled down the incline as she climbed.

Stars exploded in my eyes when I tried to stand up, a quick reminder of the tree limb sticking out of my leg. I fell on my ass again and screamed in pain.

"Luci! Wait, don't leave. Don't leave me here. I'll die out here all by myself."

She stopped climbing and turned around to look at me, hands on her hips. She didn't say anything.

"I'd already been dead without you. This whole thing is my fault."

Luci didn't move.

"What else do you want me to say? I need you. Do you want me to beg? I'll beg!"

This time she stood frozen for a few more seconds before lowering her head and shaking it. She pushed out a nasally sigh and walked back down toward me. Hallelujah! I closed my eyes and laughed out loud until my bruised ribs screamed at me to stop.

"Luci, thank you for coming back. Thank you for not leaving me. I'm so sorry. I'm not in my right mind."

"Shut up, will you? You're not right in anything. Can you even stand?" Luci asked.

I reached out and braced the tree behind me and tried to push myself up with my free arm. Those stabbing pains shot up every limb of my body again and threatened to collapse me. I felt myself straighten up and saw Luci come from behind me to catch my potential fall. I'll tell you what, she was stronger than she looked. I know I wasn't some beefcake or anything but she wasn't exactly Arnold Schwarzenegger either.

"Just be ginger with that left leg and put your weight on me," Luci said. "Getting up this hill might be a challenge."

"What are we going to do about my leg?" I asked, grimacing with every forward step.

"One of the neighbors is a veterinarian. If he's there, we'll see if he can at least patch you up."

Halfway up the hill, I had to stop and rest. My lungs felt like I was exhaling fire with every breath and then getting stabbed on the intake. Mosquitos collected on the bloodied side of my face like it was flypaper.

"Won't that be dangerous? Won't he know who I am?"

"We sure as hell can't take you to a hospital. And the other option is leaving it in and letting an infection take over," Luci said as we began to move uphill again.

"A vet sounds good," I said.

We struggled another five or so minutes up to the Buick. I slumped against the vehicle to hold myself up as Luci opened the passenger door to help me inside. Once again, I was thankful for the cloth seats but even more to be off my feet, the weight off my bastard of a leg.

Luckily the highway remained clear except for the occasional vulture streaking across the blue sky. Luci carefully buckled me in and trotted around the front of the car to her side and got in. She started the car and rolled down the windows. I turned my head to hock another ball of bloody snot and saw a patch of purple flowers, not twenty feet from where I crashed into the tree. I hadn't noticed them until now and how I wished I could smell their sweet fragrance, taste the aroma of their petals wafting through my nose.

Luci put the car in drive and we started to move forward again. I had a serene feeling that things were going to be all right. It didn't matter that my body had basically been smashed and shattered or that I needed more than just stitches or splints to help me recover. Nope, I just had a feeling that the worst of things would be past us, left down in that ditch. I watched the flowers disappear as the car rolled on and they were the last thing I saw before the blackness filled me.

# Chapter 18

It might have been the crunch of the gravel or maybe the squeal of the brakes that woke me up as Luci put the Buick in park. Either way, we stopped in a primitive driveway before a thickly wooded forest. The blood that had gushed from my brow had become tacky, making it impossible to open my left eye but I still saw well enough to know what was in front of us. The cabin.

For a moment I forgot about my injuries, my feeble attempt to bail on Luci and if I could only describe it as pure bliss, that would be enough. I looked up at the wispy clouds through the dirty windshield and thought of yesterday at the pool when this whole shebang began.

The passenger door opened.

"Come on. Let's get you inside," Luci said.

I swung my legs out of the Buick, inhaling with a sharp new sense of pain. Jesus Christ on a cracker why the hell did I jump out of the car? Luci leaned in and wrapped her arms around my midsection and helped heave me up. The car acted as a sort of resting post as I tried to compose myself.

"It's not that far to the door. Then you get to go inside and lay down while we figure out how to fix you."

The idea of walking the twenty feet to the door made me want to vomit. I winced and stepped forward, Luci beside me as we moved toward the cabin.

"Almost there," she said in a soothing teacher-like voice.

We were about halfway up the drive when the front door swung open. A man stood in the doorway, leaning against the frame. I recognized the Ret Squad uniform but didn't recognize the man. But then again, why would I?

"About time you two made it up here. Kept me waiting," the man said. I saw that he had a half-smoked cigarette in his hand. He took one more drag and put it out on the doorframe, dropping the butt onto the porch.

This was it. We had gotten this far but those bastards were indeed always one step ahead. Luci put her hand on my lower back as I leaned on her for stability.

"What the hell are you doing here?" she asked the man.

I mean, I'm no private investigator but wasn't it kind of obvious? Our luck had finally run out.

"I always forget how friendly you are, Gillespie. Kiermaier wanted me to be here when you arrived. Make sure you were okay or something I suppose." The man shrugged and scratched the back of his neck.

"Fucking Kiermaier," Luci whispered to nobody in particular.

"Luci, what is this man talking about?" I asked. My entire body began to throb, my heart rate seeming to double. I wasn't sure how much longer I was going to be able to stand.

"Luci?" the man asked, chuckling. "What are you a closet I Love Lucy fan or something?"

"Ha-ha, Darnold," Luci replied to the Ret Squad soldier. "L-U-C-I. Short for Lucifer. Thought I'd at least have some fun with it."

My head buzzed like a hornet's nest as I tried to keep up with the conversation, tried to keep up with my consciousness.

"Luci?" I tried to ask again. The sides of my vision started to fade to black.

"Sergeant Gillespie having some fun? I guess there really is a first time for everything," Darnold said.

"Luci, I don't understand what's happening. Why is he calling you Gillespie? What's going on?"

Above us, I heard a bird squawk as it tore through the sky. I couldn't lift my head to see it but met Luci's eyes instead. Or Gillespie's eyes. Or whoever the hell she was. She shook her head and rubbed her hand on my back.

"Oh shit. You mean you haven't told him?" Darnold asked. A beat of silence then Darnold, bending at his waist, clutching his gut, let out the loudest belly laugh I think I ever heard.

"Shut up and help me get him inside," Luci said, guiding me forward with her hand.

Darnold met us halfway from the door and threw his arm around my waist. I was glad to not have to bear much weight on my legs but still had no clue what was going on.

"Alright O'Malley, let's get you inside," he said.

I looked at Darnold and blinked. This guy was apparently as out of it as I was. "O'Malley is dead," I said.

"Willard is. That's right. I was there when it happened. But we still have you, Walton," Darnold said. Luci remained mum.

"My name is Ethan."

We had made it to the front porch. Now half of whatever vision I had remaining went to black.

"That's your orphan name. You've got a few things to learn my friend," Darnold said as he and Luci maneuvered me through the cabin door. "You're Walton O'Malley Jr. and this is your execution."

And then I blacked out for the second time that day.

# Chapter 19

The only other time I had ever passed out, it was on purpose. In middle school, most of the kids were playing this choking game where someone pins you against a wall or a locker or something out of the sight of the teachers and puts their palms on your throat until you hit the floor. Looking back, it was plain dumb, but I was desperate for friends, something I'd learn later in life was also plain dumb.

When I regained consciousness from the choking game, I remember a brief moment, no longer than a few seconds, where I didn't know where the hell I was at. That same feeling, I wouldn't quite call it nostalgia, filled my brain again until my eyes focused on Luci. She was sitting across the table from me drinking from an old ceramic mug.

"Welcome back. Again," she said.

I looked around trying to get my bearings. We were in what passed for a dining room, a small little nook flanked by an even smaller kitchen behind me. Beyond that, a loveseat and coffee table filled out the rest of the cabin with a door to what probably led to a bedroom just past the couch. Darnold hovered over me, smoking another cigarette.

"I'm sure you probably have some questions," Luci said.

I did.

As my mind fog started to drift away, the throbbing in my left leg replaced it. I looked down and saw a large white bandage blossoming with fresh blood where the branch that pierced my quad used to be. I still couldn't open my left eye much but my skin was free of the sticky gore that covered it after my fall. I'm sure the local mosquito population was happy about that. My entire body ached but at least now I was sitting down.

"So, this is it, huh? You're going to kill me now?" I asked.

Luci looked over my shoulder at her counterpart and said, "No, we aren't going to kill you. Darnold just likes to be dramatic."

Darnold must have taken this as a sign, or maybe he got his little feelings hurt because he and his cigarette disappeared into the living room.

"Oh, thank my lucky stars. That puts me so much more at ease," I said. I couldn't physically roll my eyes, it hurt too goddamn much, but I hoped Luci could sense my sarcasm. I never was one for theatrics anyway.

"What do you know about your parents?" Luci asked.

I closed my eyes, not to try to remember my parents but to will away the nausea that threatened to take me over. And I really didn't know anything about my parents, I went to the orphanage seconds after I breathed my first lungful of air.

"My mother died during childbirth and dear old dad put himself in the grave shortly before that."

"That's it? Did you ever know their names"?

"No. Didn't need to. I was kind of a shoo-in for the Cleanup Crew program. Don't need much family history for that job." My mouth felt like a bail of cotton. "Can I have some water?"

"We will get you something to drink in a minute."

In the middle of the table was a piece of paper. Luci slid it towards me.

"What's this?" I asked.

"A birth certificate," she said and took another sip from her mug.

I read the paper, straining to see the words. Under the live birth section, a name box listed the certificate as belonging to Walton Francis O'Malley Jr. I looked back up at Luci.

"What does this have to do with me?"

"Keep reading."

This was doing nothing for the headache that was beginning to flower behind my eyes. But I scanned the rest of the document. Time of birth was two in the afternoon. Father of the child was Walton O'Malley Sr., no surprise there. Mother was Cambria Jane O'Malley. I browsed the rest of the document, birth weight, residences, attending doctor but, again, nothing special.

"I don't see why—"

And then I saw why. At the bottom of the page was a box that only gets filled out in the event the child is given up for adoption. It lists the reason and assigns a new name to the child to make it easier for the government to track such cases. And there, in that newly assigned name box, take a guess at what I saw. If you said I saw *my* name, well good for you. Winner, winner, chicken dinner. There I was: Ethan Patrick Point.

"You're an O'Malley, Ethan," Luci said.

Well, no shit.

"Your father had two brothers. Willard you met, and Wallace you helped clean up. And that's how this all started. That's why you are here right now. But we will get to that in a minute. Your family has been an enemy of the state for a long time, Ethan. And now you are the last of its line."

My mind understood everything that Luci or Gillespie or whomever she was told me. My parents died, and I got put in the system because of it. Nothing new there. And I never wondered about my past or who I was at that point. It never interested me. But this little bomb changed all that.

"So, my parents, were they a part of all this…this rebel life savers movement?" I asked.

"That's one way to put it. Your father and Willard were thick as thieves. Wallace was more of the money man but he was smart and stayed out of most the illegal stuff."

"How did Walton…my dad, how did he…you know?"

"How did Walton die? He was protecting you and your mother. We had him on a litany of charges as your family is wont to rack up. But when we apprehended him, he wouldn't talk. Wouldn't divulge the family secrets so to speak. We almost got to him when we threatened Cambria, already eight months pregnant with you at this point. He conceded at that point and there was nowhere to run. Nowhere to go except away from himself. We found him in his cell the next morning, hanging from a makeshift bedsheet noose. And then your mother dying during childbirth, we hit a dead end. And you were assigned your government name and the rest is history."

Luci finished her cup of whatever and wiped her mouth with the back of her hand.

"Why didn't you try to go after Willard or Wallace then?" I asked.

"Willard went into hiding after he learned of your father's death. I suppose he saw the writing on the wall. And we did try to go after him. For years. It wasn't until we met you that we were able to locate him."

Fantastic. I basically killed my estranged uncle.

"It's a shame you two didn't have enough time to get to know each other. In a familial way, I mean," Luci said.

I shook my head. My eyes became wet and it started to get hard to swallow.

"Yeah, and whose fault is that?" The accusation came out weaker than I wanted. Not that it mattered anyway.

Luci smiled and continued. "Wallace, as I said, kept his nose pretty clean. We knew he was at some point financially involved but he was also a big donor every year to the Ret Squad. Money like that will protect certain people."

Should I have been more surprised about this new family history? Yes, probably. My mind likely didn't have enough time to process everything and I'm sure I had a brain injury or something from that wonderful little tumble I took from the Buick. But the thing that I relished in the most was that I wasn't alone. Not being normal, not fitting in—that was just the old family motto and so much of what I had questioned in the past made so much more damn sense now. In a way, it was beautiful.

"Is it time yet?" Darnold asked, wandering back into the dining room.

"Almost," Luci responded. "You can start getting things ready."

Darnold turned around and went back into the living room.

"What's going on in that head of yours, Ethan? I know this is a lot for you," Luci said.

I couldn't help but smile. Hot tears blinked from my eyes in steady rivulets. Their salty taste cut through the bitter copper in my mouth.

"I think it's a bit poetic," I said.

"Taking it easier than I thought."

"Not many other ways to take it, I suppose. How do *you* factor into this whole thing? At what point did the Ret Squad have my number?" I asked.

Luci looked past me into the living room at Darnold. He was taking things from a backpack and laying them out on the coffee table. I couldn't tell what any of it was.

"I deserve at least that from you," I said.

"I guess you do. I think we still have a little time."

And then Luci told me the rest of the story.

# Chapter 20

This is what Luci told me.

She told me Horatio saw me take the books from Wallace's place when we arrived for the cleanup. He saw me putting the books into my pack when this whole time I thought I had been slick enough to evade his watchful eye. And then that bastard went and told on me. He went and called the Ret Squad hotline but I guess I can't blame him. Tips leading to the apprehension of people like me, like my family, those tips get you off the cleanup crew and onto something else. Something better.

So then after Horatio's little tip, they put two rookie Ret Squad tails on me just to monitor my movements, see if they could catch me in a bigger act, I guess. But their work didn't amount to much. They never found my safe place and never found the books so they started to wean off their detail and that's when they got sloppy.

Although they had access to my online presence, something I obviously didn't know, again they didn't come across any red flags right away so they let it fall by the wayside. But if those turkeys had paid attention at all, they would have seen my dark-web search sooner and they would have realized who and what I was looking up. They would have seen the message back from the Devil's

Alphabet Society. They would have seen the plan for a rendezvous and could have followed me to where Willard and his group abducted me. These rookie officers could have tracked all that and popped the most prominent members of the Society and never worry about being promoted ever again.

Instead, by the time Tweedledee or Tweedledum decided to do their job and scan my online history again, I had already been back in my shitty little apartment dozing off on the couch. Of course, they brought my clandestine meeting up to their Lieutenant, thinking they might get some atta boys for their discovery but instead almost got demoted to a Cleanup Crew themselves.

"And that's when I came in," Luci said. She had refilled her mug with water and a wedge of lemon, still never offering me any.

"Why you?" I asked.

"The lieutenant wanted a more senior agent working the case, especially after the previous team's snafu and also the fact that this became a hot button situation. I mean, we have been trying to locate Willard and his Society for years and then he just escaped right under our noses."

It started to go dark outside, we had been in the cabin for a few hours I guess, plus whatever time I had been passed out. I couldn't see Darnold but I could hear him tinkering away on the coffee table.

"That's when I decided to do a more comprehensive look into you, Ethan. I do have to say, on the surface you are quite unremarkable." Luci paused to squeeze the lemon wedge into her mug. "But when I stumbled across your original birth certificate, boy oh boy we were cooking with fire then."

"You thought I had a connection," I said.

"At that point, I wasn't sure but I knew I needed to get you to talk to me about meeting up with Willard O'Malley. It was my plan all along to try to get you to save me. Based on the profile of you that I built, I was more than fairly certain you'd do it. Or at least try. And then we'd be bonded. And you'd have to help me. And help yourself."

She wasn't wrong. It was a damn good profile. She may have been a conniving shithead but she was good at her job.

"Problem was," Luci continued, "you hardly ever leave your apartment."

Again, she wasn't wrong.

"Almost ready in here!" Darnold shouted from the living room. He didn't really need to shout. Luci ignored him.

"So, when I decided to go to the pool, you made your move. Can you actually swim?" I asked.

"Like a duck. All my hours spent tailing you looked like they were about to pay off. I saw the opportunity and took it. I didn't even have a bathing suit or anything so I broke into a locker in the changing room. Well, actually three lockers before I found something that fit me, and went out to go drown myself," Luci said.

Boy did I feel like an idiot. I mean, I had my thoughts about Luci a little later on but how blind was I to not see *any* of this? I never really smoked but I thought about asking Darnold for a cigarette.

"And then of course you brought me back to your place, which we already knew about obviously, but I was hoping to get you to show me or lead me to the Society in some way. Instead, you brought me to your little funeral home hideout, but that was all right too because we finally found your contraband."

Luci leaned back in her chair, a smile seeming to stretch a mile wide on her face. She was definitely proud of herself.

"So, the agents banging on my apartment door, that was just to flush me out?" I asked.

"You know, that's a good way of putting it. Might have to write it up like that in my final report."

"And then they followed us to the funeral home?"

"No, I didn't want to risk looking like we were being followed. I wanted you spooked but not that paranoid. When we went to the diner, and I made that phone call, that was me calling in the location of your book stash. Or hideout or whatever."

Not that it meant anything, but I was right. She didn't have a cat. Or a dog. No call to the courteous neighbor to watch over sweet, sweet Muffin. Just a call to her Ret Squad. I started getting woozy again so I dug my thumb into my leg wound to keep myself awake. I wanted to hear the rest of the story. I needed to know how dumb I really was.

"But that trip to the diner also revealed your information about some sort of contact with 'like-minded people' so I knew I was on the right track. Having the Ret Squad come in and canvas your funeral home was just the spark needed to have you lead me to the Society," Luci said.

And probably lead her to a big fat bonus too.

"It was the only option I had left," I said, then felt even more stupid trying to defend myself.

"Either way, you led us right where I wanted to be."

I sat in silence for a few beats, thinking about the trip to the compound.

"And that's why you wanted my phone."

"Hey, you're catching on," Luci said. "I'm lucky you still had battery and we still had signal but it was enough to drop the GPS coordinates to my Ret Squad commander so they could set up the siege. Now that didn't really go as planned. I didn't think ol' Willard would blow himself up, but here we are."

If I had a gun right then, and knew how to use it, I would have shot Luci right in her stupid stomach. I would have watched her bleed out and I would have asked Darnold for a smoke.

"Why didn't you just turn me into the Ret Squad when they raided the compound? Why did you wake me up and feign like you wanted to talk to me at the river?" I asked.

"Because you're special. You're a different case than that whole compound thing. You're mine and I'm going to see you through right to the end," Luci replied.

I felt so special, let me tell you. Special like a three-dollar bill.

"So, the plan was to get me up to this cabin all along?" I asked.

"For the most part. Just needed you to get me to O'Malley first. After I dropped the compound coordinates to my contact, I also had them leave me a car to switch out of behind that Waffle Palace. I was actually going to suggest we ditch the piece of shit car we stole earlier for a different ride, you know, keep up the charade of not wanting to get caught, but you beat me to it. It was kind of perfect actually."

So perfect that I just ended up playing a character in her little play. An idiot in three acts. And now it was almost time for the curtain call.

"I'm guessing this isn't your parent's cabin then," I said.

"Bingo. This property belongs to the State and the Ret Squad uses it quite a bit for little operations here and there. It's quite charming, don't you think?" Luci gulped the last of her water and looked around the small cabin. Her Cheshire grin still plastered onto her stupid face.

"I guess you got me then. Congratulations," I said.

"Don't feel too bad, Ethan. You were onto me at the end. I really thought I had screwed up. I thought you made me."

So close. So close, but what could I have actually done anyway? I shook my head.

"You obviously didn't leave me to die in the ditch when I bailed on the Buick, so what's next? Take me in and put me in the gas chamber? Maybe a firing squad? Do I at least get to choose?"

A loud laugh spurted from Luci's mouth. Darnold, still in the living room chuckled as he kept at whatever he was doing.

"I told you, Ethan. This isn't an execution and the Ret Squad doesn't kill people. I don't know what stories you've heard. Murder is still a crime."

"What then? Do I get to go in front of a judge? Am I going to prison?"

Luci tried to hold her laughter in this time but failed. Probably the only thing she had failed at in the small amount of time that I knew her.

"Oh no," she said, wiping tears from her eyes, "nothing like that either. You broke the law. You attempted to save someone. There are consequences and there needs to be a *balance*. There needs to be *retribution*. There's no judge to prove your innocence to because you aren't innocent."

"Sounds like bullshit entrapment to me," I said. I was really grasping at straws now.

"Whatever makes you sleep at night."

"So, what now then?"

"Now it's time for retribution. We don't kill you. You kill you," Luci said.

Darnold had snuck up behind me again, holding a cup of some kind of liquid.

"Get up and follow me."

# Chapter 21

I hear Luci and Darnold walk back into the kitchen. I'm in the bedroom across from the living room, the door is open and I see Darnold breaking apart big white capsules, dumping their powdery innards into a glass. This is the end, my only friend, the end.

I see Luci hand Darnold another cup, half full with water. They are my gods now and I'm finally going to get my drink.

I feel my tongue stick to the roof of my mouth as Darnold yells from the kitchen. He says the cocktail he's making, it's the same thing they give the terminally ill and the destitute when it's time to send them to their endless slumber. He mixes the water and the powder with a plastic spork.

I smell, through the half-open bedroom window, the rain coming. My crew used to tease me about that skill, predicting precipitation by the aroma. It will rain soon, but I'm not sure if I'll be alive when it comes.

I'm sitting here now, on the edge of this bed. Darnold is standing near the door when Luci walks in carrying my cocktail. It looks like watery milk. She holds it out to me and asks if I understand what it is.

I tell her yes.

She asks if I understand what it will do.

I tell her it will kill me.
She tells me I have to drink all of it.
I drink the entire glass.
It tastes like wood

# Epilogue- 9 Months Later

"Get this fucking thing out of me!" Luci screamed. Her knuckles turned as white as bleached bone from gripping the sheets on the bed. Her hospital gown clung to her body like a wetsuit. Sweat cascaded down from her temples and her hair plastered the side of her face.

"Ma'am, I just need you to push one more time, really big for me. Can you do that?" the delivery doctor asked, peeking over Luci's bent knees.

If Luci had her way, this pregnancy would have been aborted the minute she found out about it. But as she knew with all her years of handing out retribution, murder was wrong and abortion was murder.

"Ahhhh!" Luci screamed into the room. Her breaths came in laboring hitches, Lamaze classes be damned. "Get it out!"

The baby was going to be a breech birth but Luci wasn't concerned about that. She was concerned with getting the whole production over and done with and alleviating the most excruciating pain she had ever felt in her life.

"Almost there," the doctor said as he maneuvered the umbilical cord so as not to damage it as Luci pushed.

And then the sweet wailing cries of a newborn filled the room. The attending nurses applauded at the sound of the baby's brays as the doctor readied the child for some skin-to-skin contact time with its mother. He wiped the birthing gore from the baby's face and body, making sure to keep the nasal passages clear then bent down to place the child on Luci's chest.

"That won't be necessary, doctor," a nurse said and pointed to Luci's heart rate monitor. Sometime between the last push and the baby extraction, the machine had flatlined. The doctor handed the baby off to the nurse and checked the pulse on Luci's wrist. Nothing.

A hospital staffer walked in shortly thereafter with a paper in his hand.

"Doctor, can you please review the baby's birth certificate and sign it?" the staffer asked.

The doctor scanned the sheet for the father's name.

"Is the father here?" he looked for the name on the paper. "Uh…an Ethan Pointe?"

"I'm afraid he's deceased, doctor," the staffer responded.

They both looked back to Luci's cooling corpse on the blood-soaked hospital bed.

"I see. Will you please call the State so we can get the process started on getting this little guy into the system?" the doctor said, looking at the crying baby in the nurse's arms.

"Yes doctor, I'll call them right away," the staffer said.

The doctor signed the birth certificate then checked a box down toward the bottom labeled "eligible for adoption". He gave it back to the staffer and the staffer disappeared down the hall. The doctor retrieved the baby from the nurse and held it out in his hands, eye to eye.

"I'm sorry little guy. Life is already difficult enough, but for you, it just got tougher."

The baby continued to cry.

# Author's Note & Bonus Story

Well, well, well. Here we are again. I hope you enjoyed the weird and twisted tale of Ethan and Luci. I started writing *The Cleanup Crew* in Early 2020 but lost the file in a computer crash that erased a few months of work. Although I was pretty devastated by it (folks, don't forget to back up your files!), I decided to sit down and hammer out as much as I could remember and continue the story. I'm glad I did.

I never had a clear ending in mind, figuring it would work itself out in time, but one night I was going over some flash fiction I had stashed away and BOOM! It hit me. Like with my last book, *A Haunt of Travels*, I included a bonus story and I'd like to do the same here. But we will get to that in a minute…

First, I want to talk about something that has affected my life on a deep level and is discussed in *The Cleanup Crew* as well. I don't add trigger warnings to my books, I can appreciate my fellow authors that do, but that's just not me I suppose. To me, art can be a painfully beautiful experience and genres like horror and terror and suspense can do such a wonderful job of exploring traumas like grief, depression or death. My dad died from suicide almost two decades ago and is also the man to whom this book is dedicated. He's still very much a huge part of who I am and how I go about my own life. In *The Cleanup Crew*, the theme of suicide is explored in several different facets, and in a way, writing about it helps me to understand it better.

As with *A Haunt of Travels*, I pledge to donate a portion of my profits from this book to a cause I've been involved with in the past and am grateful for the work that they do. That organization is the American Foundation for Suicide Prevention (afsp.org). I encourage all my readers to check them out and look at the work they do for local communities. Mental illness is a bastard creature that doesn't care about your race, gender or socio-economic background (or if you refuse to use the Oxford comma). Because of that, it is something we should all feel strongly about. Ending the stigma surrounding it and supporting the folks that are working to make that happen is the least we can do.

Another theme that is explored in *The Cleanup Crew* is death and how we as a society respond to it. I was taking a class for my degree, a class called Communication at the End of Life, and we watched a documentary about the Death with Dignity laws up in the Pacific Northwest. If you haven't heard about it, it's an interesting case study in medical morality and ethics coinciding with human morality and ethics. The documentary inspired me to write a piece of flash fiction and after rediscovering it on my hard drive, it also inspired the ending to this book.

It's funny how these things work sometimes, but I'll take the serendipity however it comes. I hope you enjoy the story and how it helped shape *The Cleanup Crew*.

# The Empty Glass

I hear the doctor walk into my kitchen.  She sits down at the small breakfast nook and begins breaking apart big white capsules and dumps their powdery innards into a glass.  I have cancer and I live in Oregon.  Those are two things you should know about me.  And please, spare me your bullshit platitudes; they don't apply now and didn't apply two years ago when I thought I had this nasty thing licked.  It took me until recently to realize this sickness and I wasn't destined for a restitution narrative.  I'm not going to get better and if I hadn't chosen today to die, I'd only last a few more weeks, at most, anyway.

I see my wife, Julia, hand the doctor another glass, half full of water.  She didn't speak to me for close to a week after I made this decision.  I struggled with the morality of it.  At first, even with all the pain and suffering I had already endured, would continue to endure until I could no longer breathe on my own, I was on the fence about enacting my right to die.  How could I be so arrogant as to decide when my time was *my time*?  I'm certainly not God.

I feel my daughter's hand guide me to the edge of my bed as we wait for Julia and the doctor.  Oregon is a "Death with Dignity" state.  I admit I was ignorant of its purpose until my doctor billed it as an alternative to my prolonged suffering. I already decided I wasn't going to do the treatment again, and my family, as much as they initially pressed back, now supports me. It seems they're more afraid of losing me than I am of leaving them. In a strange way, I appreciate that. My doctor helped me fill out the necessary forms, much of it bureaucratic nonsense, but now she's in my kitchen, mixing the cocktail I will drink to put me into an everlasting slumber.

I smell, through the open bedroom window, the rain coming. My neighbor teases me about that skill, predicting precipitation by the aroma. His wife died from leukemia five years ago. Right after my own cancer came back, he stopped over to help me install a new water heater. He told me something that changed my perception of "Death with Dignity" when I was having my own reservations about the practice. He said his wife begged him for days during her last month to kill her, put her out of her pain. He wishes he would have listened. The chaos of this cancer has already taken so much from me and it was then I decided that it was not going to also take my autonomy. My life *is* my life and my family, again after some debate, understands that too.

I'm sitting here now, on the edge of my bed. My wife joins me, lightly stroking my back. My daughter is standing near the door when the doctor walks in carrying my cocktail. It looks like watery milk. She holds it out to me and asks if I want to change my mind about taking it.

I tell her no.

She asks if I understand what it will do.

I tell her it will kill me.

She tells me I have to drink all of it.

I drink the entire glass.

It tastes like wood.

# Thank You

An idea doesn't become a book without a team of people pitching in and making sure I don't run this thing off the rails. Because of that, I have some folks to salute. First, thanks to my editor, Aubrie Orr, for once again polishing up all these words and providing excellent insight into the world I was trying to build. Thank you to my early readers, Alana K. Drex, Beth Griffith and Lydia Koster for taking the time to read through and impart their unique wisdom. Thanks to my family for their everlasting love and support as well as Mae Morel and Kristina Swoboda for their steadfast encouragement. Finally, Dear Reader, thanks to you for taking a chance on me and on this book.

# About the Author

A.W. Mason lives in Florida with his cat Wallace, a retired extreme parkour artist (who looks so dapper in his little helmet and knee pads). He enjoys great beer, all the nachos and constantly tries to convince himself he actually likes running.

He is a graduate of the University of South Florida with a degree in communications, whatever that is.

His first book, *A Haunt of Travels*, is a short story collection with tales of horror, terror, suspense, crime and science fiction. Mason is working on a few projects, one a new book tentatively titled *What Happened in the Sugarmill Woods* as well as an untitled Werewolf novella.

*Oh hey, you're still here. I suppose you'd like a reward or something? Well, you're in luck…*

"All right O'Malley, put down the detonator and come back outside with us. There's nowhere to go," Ret Squad agent Tillman said.

Willard stepped back as Tillman and Boreno trained their rifles on him. Neither agent saw the man in the corner with his own firearm. Neither agent heard the silenced pistol discharge two rounds, two perfect headshots. The agents fell lifeless to the ground.

"Good work, Lenny," Willard said. "Let's get the hell out of here and round up as many others as we can."

Lenny nodded and kicked a rug away from the center of the floor. He flipped up and pulled a handle, lifting a small plate in the ground and watched as Wallace descended into a manmade tunnel. Lenny followed after, lowering the steel plate.

A safe distance down the tunnel, Willard flipped a switch on the detonator, turning a light at the top green. He looked to Lenny once again, both men nodding as O'Malley pushed a flat silver button. The ground trembled, cascading them with loose dirt as the building somewhere above them exploded.

**Willard O'Malley and the Devil's Alphabet Society will return…**

Printed in Great Britain
by Amazon